Cottage of Secrets

Ron Walters

Published 2015 by arima publishing

www.arimapublishing.com

ISBN 978 1 84549 649 4
© Ron Walters 2015

Printed and bound in the United Kingdom

Typeset in Garamond

Swirl is an imprint of arima publishing.

arima publishing
ASK House, Northgate Avenue
Bury St Edmunds, Suffolk IP32 6BB
t: (+44) 01284 700321
www.arimapublishing.com

Acknowledgement

Many thanks to my friend John Young

Chapter 1

Frank and Beth Haines sat enjoying their breakfast when their two children, Maisie aged ten and Lewis twelve, came running into the room. The children were so excited because they were all going away today for one week's holiday. Beth had found a French Farm Cottage advertised on the internet and she thought it would be ideal for a family holiday and it would give Frank some time to rest, so she had booked it.

Beth was very concerned about Frank's health, he had been working seven days a week and long hours over the past few months and she thought it would be a perfect holiday. She had tried to get Frank to work fewer hours but he wouldn't. It was not as if they were desperate for the money, they each had inherited money from a distant relative. Frank being a joiner his services was always in demand.

They had made a reservation in a Dover hotel for a family room tonight. They both thought the children would settle better if the journey was broken up and they would not get overtired and irritable. Frank brought the car round to the back of the house to load and as is normal the children wanted to take all their electrical gadgets with them. He got very bad tempered as the children would not listen to reason. Beth had to step in as the peace maker.

The children did not realize that their father was apprehensive about driving on the right hand side of the road as opposed to this country and this did make him a little irritable. He programmed his Satellite Navigation to the address of the cottage ready for when they landed in Calais.

The family got into the car whilst Frank went round house checking that all the doors and windows were locked, once checked, they set off on their holidays. Frank was a little concerned leaving the house at the present time; there had been so many break-ins and squatters moving into property with very little help from the police to have them removed.

The excitement bubbled over and the children started falling out and arguing, once again Beth had to play the part of peace maker, a thing mothers do well.

When they arrived at the hotel in Dover, Frank decided to leave the luggage in the car overnight but the young lady on the reception desk advised against it, it is obvious who had the job of unloading the car as the children were too excited, Beth managed to keep some sort of control over them.

When Frank had finished unloading the car and the family had helped to take the luggage to their bedroom they decided to eat.

The family got freshened up and went down to find the dining room. Lewis ordered his usual burger and chips. Both of his parents had tried to persuade him to try a different meal but without success. The family sat talking and discussing what lies ahead of them, Lewis started asking all sorts of questions. What if the ferry sinks with their car on board and again Beth stepped in because it was upsetting Maisie.

When the ferry arrived at Calais, Beth had difficulty trying to calm the children's excitement while watching the crew wrestling with the mooring cables as the ferry docked. Frank ushered his family to the lower level and looked around until they found their car, they all got into the car and got seated. They had to wait patiently for instructions from a seaman, who was in control of the disembarking of all the vehicles. The seaman waved to Frank indicating he was to go down the slope onto the dock area which led him to the main roads leading from the docks.

As Frank joined the main road, he activated his "Satellite Navigation" which had been programmed earlier.

The roads were much quieter than Frank had expected but he still had a little difficulty negotiating the roundabouts it was just as well the roads were quiet, this gave him a little more time to get in the right position.

After driving several miles and dealing with a number of roundabouts, he suddenly felt comfortable driving on the opposite side of the road.

They had been travelling for nearly two hours when they entered a small village and the voice on the Sat Nav: told Frank to turn right down a small lane, they travelled about 300 yards passing a large farm house on their right-hand side. They reached the end of the road where there was a circle of eight detached cottages, each with their own small garden. Frank drove slowly and a voice from the instrument said,

"You have reached you destination."

Beth pointed out number four which is the cottage they are going to be staying in but they had to collect the key from number six.

Beth got out of the car and went and knocked on the door of number six and a young lady opened the door.

"Hello, can I help you?"

"Yes, I hope so, my name is Beth Haines, I have rented cottage number four for one week and I understand that you are the key holder?"

"Yes, do come in and meet my husband Bob, he will take you across and show you round."

"My family is in the car, you must meet them."

"Bring them in; I'll put the kettle on."

Beth went back to the car and asked them to join her and meet Mr. and Mrs. Styles. Frank and the children entered the house.

*

"Have you had a good journey Frank?"

"As well as my rowdy children allowed me to, he said laughing. The trip was quite straight forward, arrangements on the ferry were very well organized; of course, it is a daily task to the seamen."

"Yes, it can be difficult having distraction while driving on strange roads but children completes one's life. Now would you like a scotch or a glass of wine, I know the ladies would prefer tea, or they might indulge in a G&T," he winked at Frank "the children can have some of Mary's fruit juice."

Frank felt quite at ease with Bob and his wife.

When they had finished their drinks, Bob handed Frank the key to the cottage.

"Come along I'll show you round, the rooms may be smaller than you are used to but these cottages are cozy and comfortable."

Bob unlocked the door and when they went into the cottage Beth immediately felt relaxed, looking across at Frank, she knew he felt the same.

The lounge had a wood burning stove and a comfortable settee, two armchairs, two smaller upholstered chairs, TV and a radio. They moved into the kitchen, which, was quite small but well laid out, everything was close to hand and there appeared to be plenty of cooking utensils laid out on a gas oven and hob.

One thing Beth checked, it had running water. Her friends had teased her about no running water and a dry toilet.

Going up the stairs, they found one large master bedroom and two smaller bedrooms, which, had once been a large room but had been partitioned to create the two rooms. Beth checked the beds and she was delighted to find them so comfortable, she turned to Mary.

"This is great, just what I wanted to give Frank a rest."

When they went down stairs, Mary showed them where a small extension had been built at the back of the cottage to create a bathroom consisting of a shower and a toilet. Bob turned to Lewis.

"Do you fish?"

"No, I've never tried."

"Right, we will take your father with us and we will go fly fishing. Firstly, I'll show you how to make a colourful fly to lure the fish on to the hook and hopefully we can catch some trout from the river just beyond the farm. Fly fishing is quite an art but it is a challenging sport. My lad Dan thinks he is good but I still come home with a heavier bag. He and I have a wonderful relationship, we argue and we both know best, or think we do, so it ends up as a draw. Incidentally, Dan and his sister Sam will be back in a few days, they are spending some time with their Grandma. Samantha answers to her nickname Sam, Dan first called her Sam when she was very young and it has stuck."

Bob helped Frank unload the car and take the luggage indoors; it was obvious that Bob and Mary were pleased to have some company.

The whole family was having a fantastic week; Beth had never seen the children so happy and contented. They all enjoyed visiting the small village, the different cultures and the quaint café bars they found exciting, especially in the evening. Beth could see she would have trouble when it came time to pack their cases to return home.

*

Frank, Beth and family were invited by Bob and Mary to a meal two days before they were due to return home. They were surprised when the meal was served, it was trout and they were told the fish had been caught by Lewis, his head expanded. Frank had been fishing with Bob and Lewis; he couldn't understand how they had kept the secret from him but he was delighted for Lewis.

During the evening the conversation drifted to their return home in two days' time, not one of them was looking forward to the return journey. Maisie looked across at Bob.

"Mr. Styles, How much money would it cost me to buy the boarded up cottage opposite?"

They all looked startled and the room erupted with laughter.

"Have you got money we don't know about Maisie," said Bob chuckling "I am not too sure Maisie; it was boarded up when we moved here five years ago, it is said that it has been empty for around ten years, maybe more. The estate agent has left a key with me but I'm not aware of any enquiries. I don't know the full history but it is rumoured that the cottage was the centre for the local French resistance groups but that is hearsay. The reason it was closed and boarded up because no one is sure to whom it belongs.

The story goes that the husband and wife who lived there were both shot by the Gestapo but as I said before, it's all hearsay.

Would you like me to unlock the door and show you around the cottage tomorrow morning?" Bob had a job to keep a straight face.

"Oh! Yes please Mr. Styles."

"Frank, will you come across and help me remove some of the boards from the windows to let some daylight into the rooms?"

"Certainly, give me a shout when you intend going across to the cottage." The following morning, Frank and Bob removed several boards to let in some daylight, Frank turned round and saw that both families were walking across; they didn't want to be left out.

Bob unlocked the door and they all walked inside cottage number two, Beth looked at Frank, what a terrible mess she thought, there were plates still laid on the table and among the dirt and dust on the floor were broken glasses.

The first impression was shock but the more Beth looked the more her mind ticked over, in fact, she began to think it had potential and what a challenge it could be.

"Yes dad lets buy it." Frank turned to Maisie.

"How can we buy it, we don't know the asking price and it would need a lot of restoration."

"That is your job dad" said Lewis smiling.

Beth had already plans in her mind to face up to such a challenge but how could they spend the time here to carry out the necessary work.

"How much are they asking for this cottage Bob?"

"I am not sure, as I told you last night; it has been boarded up for five years to our knowledge. I bet they would be more than ready to negotiate a price, to get it off their books."

The main room had a wood burning inglenook fireplace and it was covered in rubbish and dust, it looked awful.

When Beth looked in the kitchen, she shuddered, turning to Frank.

"The kitchen units will need pulling out and replaced with modern units." As Beth said that, her mind started ticking.

"No Frank, just replace the worktops and paint the unit doors and replace the old cooking range with an Aga cooker and we can run controlled central heating from the Aga."

When they investigated the power supplies, they found they would need to have two large Calor Gas Cylinders to feed the gas and the electricity would need reconnecting.

"Frank, if you do decide to go ahead, I would advise you to get the cylinders supplied from the village rather than one of the big boys, they might offer them at a little cheaper price but use the village people as much as you can. Take this advice to heart, by using them to make a living you will be accepted as a member of the village."

"Thanks Bob, that sounds like good advice."

Finally after Frank had made notes and taken measurements to carry out any repairs and alterations, should they decide to make an offer, both families went into the village with one purpose in mind, to get some idea of the property prices.

After looking in the windows of the two estate offices, Beth and Frank had formed a figure in their mind should they make an offer, at present they were undecided but they were sold on the area.

It was a tearful farewell as they left Mary and Bob the following day. Before they left, Mary and Beth hugged, surprising how they had become close friends after just one week. They exchanged addresses and telephone numbers.

"When we decide to make an offer I'll get Frank to phone Bob, he has offered to help, I feel sure we shall see you again very soon."

Chapter 2

The journey home was quite uneventful in spite of the increased amount of traffic all heading towards Calais. The traffic was mainly the heavy duty vehicles on their way to catch the ferry to deliver their goods to the UK. He was a little upset having to pay money called "Toll money" to travel on the French roads when these heavy continental Lorries pay nothing on the UK roads, he thought it a little unfair.

They decided not to stay overnight in a hotel on their return journey, once they were away from the docks in Dover, Beth took over the driving to give Frank a break, she was quite comfortable driving on her home ground.

When they arrived home, they were all very tired and ready for bed. Frank was a little weary of constantly being badgered all the way home about buying the small cottage they had visited.

However, the following evening while having dinner, Frank told the children that he and their mother had decided to put in a silly offer for the cottage just to test the market. The children were delighted to be told that their parents were thinking their way. Beth told them that the cost of restoration would be about the same as the buying price, the stumbling block is the time factor and it would be a lot easier if the cottage was around the corner when they could spend some time doing jobs during a week-end or a small job one evening.

That evening Frank telephoned Bob asking him to submit his offer of 16,000 Euro's for the cottage to the estate agent and point out the cost involved cleaning and modernizing the cottage.

The following evening Frank received a call from Bob telling him that the agent is looking for 22.000 Euro's but I think you ought to be able to negotiate a price with him.

"Right Bob, I will go to 18.000 based on the currency exchange rate today, which is varying on the euro's to the pound, it would be approximately £15,000, that figure is my ceiling, bearing in mind the cost and time it will take to make the property habitable again."

"Okay Frank, I will pop into the estate office in the morning and I'll tell him you want a prompt reply otherwise you are going to consider another property you had viewed while you were here. He will have to consult the company who is responsible for the disposing of the property."

Two evenings later Bob phoned with the good news, they would accept Franks revised offer and he gave Frank the details of the French solicitor who will deal with the details of the sale. The following day Frank contacted his solicitor and deposited £2,000 to get the deal underway. He would pay the final amount plus the solicitor's fee when it was requested.

Ten days elapsed and Frank received a phone call from his solicitor asking him to call at his office as he had the papers ready for him to sign, which would make him the owner of the French Cottage. Frank phoned and made an appointment, he went along signed the papers, paid all the money that was due, which, was the balance on the purchase of the cottage plus the solicitors fee for dealing with the transfer. He was very surprised when the solicitor told him that the freehold property would be his in seven days' time.

*

Frank and Beth sat down one evening to have a serious discussion on how to approach the restoration of the cottage. They agreed that Frank should go alone for one week to create some sort of order in the kitchen and the sleeping areas. When the children break up from school for their six weeks holiday, they can all go and really get cracking at the cottage and turn it into their home.

Bob rang to enquire if there had been any movement. "I am pleased to say the sale has gone through and I am coming over for one week."

Will you enquire in the village if one of the stores can supply the Aga Cooker, radiators and Formica worktops for the kitchen? If not I will bring the tops with me."

Frank was delighted when Bob told him that Mary and he had been into the cottage and cleaned it right through but not in depth.

"In other words, you have taken off the top layers of dirt and dust off in the general area."

"You have got it in one Frank, if you tell me when you are arriving, I will arrange for the cooker to be delivered plus a plumber come gas fitter on the second day that should allow you time to deal with the kitchen tops, which, you will bring with you. If you have any sense Frank, let Beth select the colour", this made them both laugh.

The date Frank intended going was decided on and he phoned Bob to enable him to make arrangements at his end. Frank had to rearrange his work schedule and he checked his list of measurements, tools and fittings. His vehicle is a station wagon so he was able to load the worktops in comfortably.

The morning he set off was a tearful one, Beth did not like the idea of being left behind, in the past; it was wherever one went the other went too. Frank enjoyed the journey but he did not like travelling without Beth.

When he arrived, Bob and Mary made him very welcome and he spent a pleasant evening with them and their children Dan and Sam.

Frank had taken a sleeping bag with him as he intended to sleep in the cottage but Mary would not hear of it, he snuggled down in his sleeping bag in their cottage.

Bob suggested that they should unload Frank's car and put the worktops and tools under lock and key in the cottage.

Frank was up bright and early; his intention was to go down into the village for his breakfast later but Mary had other plans. He went to the cottage to make a start; he had just got the old worktops off when Mary shouted him that his breakfast was ready for him. During breakfast, he discussed the kitchen lay out and Frank decided not to install the new tops until the Aga had been delivered, positioned and fitted.

The next job he decided to work on after breakfast was the windows in the master bedroom, they were jammed and would not open and he was unsure whether or not they had been screwed up to make the cottage secure and prevent intruders. He was confident, after a couple of hours he would have all the windows upstairs, opening and closing.

After enjoying a delicious breakfast, Frank went back to his cottage to continue working, carried the old worktops outside and left them on the grass, he would attend to them later.

He and Bob had previously discussed that he should delay fitting the worktops until the Aga had been delivered, positioned and plumbed to accept the gas to supply the domestic and heating water. He painted the unit doors a mushroom colour but the colour of the walls he decided to leave until Beth arrives. Having got the kitchen ready to receive the Aga, he decided to have a look at the bedrooms. As he climbed the stairs he glanced up and saw a damp patch on the ceiling in the master bedroom, he decided to investigate as this could develop into a larger problem.

*

Normally, there is a small dropdown door from the ceiling to allow access into the loft but he could not find it, he decided to visit Bob's cottage as they all appear to have been built from the same plans. He went across to Bob's cottage and he showed Frank the position of the trapdoor, Frank measured and made a mental note of its position and went back to his cottage.

Frank went into the room where he stored all his tools and equipment; he picked up his step ladders and went upstairs. He proceeded to push and shove against ceiling in the area Bob's trapdoor was situated, eventually he found it; it had been cleverly fitted so as not to look obvious to a casual glance.

His mind started ticking, I wonder what is hidden in the loft, he went up the steps and climbed into the loft, he shone his powerful electric lamp round and he was surprised, the floor had been boarded and under the flooring soil had been put between the rafters to act as insulation. Frank was a little puzzled but he was told this is the method of insulation that is often used by the French in the farming areas. From the ceiling beams to the floor the walls had been boarded with sheets of plywood, to create a comfortable room.

Looking round he saw a bundle of clothing rolled up in a ball in one corner, as he unrolled the bundle and found three RAF tunics, each had the pilot's wings sewn on the breast of the jackets. The bands around the sleeves indicated that one was a sergeant pilot and the other two were officers. He looked carefully at the uniforms and the names and rank was printed on a label inside pocket, they were Sergeant Worley, Flying Officer Hanlon and Pilot Officer Franks. The two officers had ribbons sewn on the breast indicating they had been awarded the DFC. Frank was wondering whether they got back home after being helped by the people who had been living here and perhaps shot for hiding them, it could be true; this cottage was used by the resistance groups. He decided not mention his find, he put the tunics in his car. He was very fortunate; he was able to slide the offending loose roofing tile back into place and seal it without having to climb on to the roof. Hoping this would solve the damp patch problem.

*

The Aga arrived the third day, a day late. The Aga was too heavy to be manhandled; the two men used rollers to slide the cooker off the lorry and to position the cooker in the kitchen. They levered the cooker into the position Frank wanted and the men set to, plumbing the water system for the domestic and heating, when they were satisfied with that, they rolled, two large calor gas cylinders from the lorry and put them by the outside wall of the kitchen and connected the gas supply. Frank was very impressed how workmanlike and efficient the men were. They lit the stove to ensure there were no leaks of gas or water and they promised to call the following day to make a further check to be sure everything was sealed correctly, it was arranged that Frank would pay them when they called next day. They did call as they had promised, obviously the fact that Frank had promised to pay them cash for their work and materials, this made sure they returned.

Frank was delighted, when the workmen lit the Aga, after a few minutes there was hot water to the domestic taps and when they switched on the circulating pump, the radiators started to get warm. Frank went round with the workmen's boss to ensure there were no leaks on any of the joints, when the boss handed Frank the bill, he paid, they shook hands and the workmen left, taking all the packing rubbish with them.

Frank was very pleased with his progress but he was determined to check the large wooden bed in the master bedroom, it was too heavy for him to move himself, he decided to wait until Bob returned from the village. When he saw Bob's car arriving, he went across and asked for his help. "Come in for a coffee before we start work Frank."

Chapter 3

Frank and Bob sat at the dining table enjoying their coffee, Frank explained to Mary and Bob that he was going to replace the mattresses and the beds, he thought they looked dirty and he was unsure what bugs might be hiding there, just waiting to feast on any warm body that should lie down. They both agreed with him, although it will upset Frank's plans a little.

Mary offered to go with Frank to buy the new beds and bedding and she would deal with the delivery when Frank had returned home.

After coffee they went across to the cottage and went upstairs, the first thing they did was to lift the bedding off the bed frames and pushed them through the windows and they landed on the small lawn at the back, they dismantled the wooden beds and lifted them on to the landing. When they had moved the large bed frame, they could see droppings which indicated that vermin was or had been present.

"Don't worry about the vermin Frank; we will bring a couple of the farmer's cats to stay for a couple of days, they are quite experienced dealing with the vermin in the barns."

Frank was kneeling down on the floor studying at patch of the floor boards.

"What is bothering you Frank?"

"I'm not bothered," he could see the wooden tongues were not engaged in the grooves for quite a way. With that, he prised up a square section of the wooden flooring and lifting his flashlight, he spotted a small dirty canvas bag. Using a long pole he dragged the bag to within his reach, as he picked up the bag, he was showered with dirt and dust, he took it to an open window and he banged and shook it outside. When he opened the bag, they looked at each other in amazement. There were six bundles of bank notes, when they checked and counted they found that each bundle contained 1,000 francs. They put four bundles back in the canvas bag and decided to take their find to the police station.

"Bob, is the French law the same as ours, you can be done for stealing by finding?" They both burst out laughing.

*

When they arrived at the police station, Frank and Bob explained to the policeman on duty how and where they had been found, it was a comedy scene with the two languages being mangled in an effort to understand each other. The duty policeman took the bag and with the help of two colleagues counted the bundles. When the counting was completed, the policeman looked at Bob.

"Is this all?"

"The bag is just as we found it"

The duty policeman looked up and smiled.

"I will give you a receipt for four thousand Francs, if it is not claimed in six months, it is yours."

Bob patted Frank on his shoulder. The kids can have the 2000 for a scrapbook.

"Come along we will go into Pierre's for a coffee and a cognac" and they ran down the street like a couple of schoolboys laughing as they ran.

"Bob, have you spoken to the farmer about borrowing two of his barn cats?"

"Yes, we can call for them on the way home but I would suggest we empty all the rooms of any furniture you don't intend keeping before we put the cats in"

That evening Frank telephoned Beth and explained the situation and it was decided that Frank should stay until everything was organized.

During the evening meal at Bob's house, they each told funny stories against themselves and they all jumped when the telephone started to ring. Mary picked up the receiver, she turned to Bob. "It's for you." He was on the telephone for quite a while, when he returned to the table, he turned to Frank. "Your furniture will have to go on the back burner, the company I am a consultant for has a welding problem on one of their oilrigs they want me there tomorrow lunchtime."

*

The following morning Frank sat finishing his breakfast, he decided to dismantle the old beds into as small pieces as possible so he can get them down the stairs. As he was struggling down the stairs he suddenly became aware of the back end was being lifted, he looked round and he saw a boy wearing jeans, jersey and a baseball cap and the boy was lifting the back end and between them they got it out on to the back garden.

Without any hesitation, the boy walked back into the cottage and mounted the stairs and indicated to Frank that he would help him carry the big old bedstead downstairs. Not a word was spoken and when they got all the bed frames outside, Frank said.

"Would you like a cup of coffee?"

The boy didn't answer, Frank got two cups out of the cupboard and pointed to the coffee pot, the boy nodded his head. Frank made the coffee and put the cup on the table and pushed a chair up to the table.

Instead of sitting down, the boy put his fingers to his lips and went out the back door, Frank was mystified, one minute later the boy walked back in carrying a bottle, when the boy held the bottle under a running tap to clean the bottle, he could read the label "Brandy" which, surprised Frank, as Brandy was referred to as Cognac in this part of the country.

When the boy had got all the dirt and filth off the bottle, he opened it and poured the liquid into two glasses he got from the cupboard. The boy raised his glass, clinked it against Frank's glass.

When Frank took a sip of the Brandy from the glass, he was amazed; he had never tasted any Brandy or Cognac to equal it.

The boy raised his hand and Frank took it and they shook hands. Frank started speaking to him but the boy pointed to his ears and his mouth shaking his head, he couldn't speak or hear he then removed his baseball cap. He had a very deep scar above his left eye going round to the back of his head and his mouth was twisted; it looked as if a bullet had gone through one cheek and out of the other.

In fact, Frank immediately felt very sorry for the boy, he was badly disfigured and his appearance would offend a lot of unsympathetic people. The boy could not smile but his eyes were full of friendly laughter, he placed his hand on Frank's shoulder gently pulling him to follow him.

Frank thought, why not. They walked a while until they came to a row of small houses behind the Farmhouse, quite close to the river Frank and Lewis had been fishing.

They approached one of the houses; the young boy knocked on the door and walked in to the house. He came back out accompanied by a short rotund lady who waddled through the door to where Frank was standing, whatever her appearance, her face was covered with a most gorgeous smile and laughing eyes, which, made her a beautiful and attractive lady. She started speaking to Frank in French which Frank did not understand.

A gentleman popped his head around the door and spoke to Frank in English.

"Please come in."

Looking at the man Frank said.

"You speak English language fluently."

"Yes, during the war I was stationed on a Free French Airfield in Lincolnshire for two years. I must explain to you, this young man is deaf and dumb.

Early one morning, Madame Fleur was out collecting mushrooms when she found Jacque, which is what we named him, beneath a hedgerow covered in blood barely alive. She carried him back here and has cared for him the past seven years. He has become a loving caring young man and in spite of his disability and disfigurement the whole village is very kind to him."

"Have you had his hearing and speech investigated by a medical practitioner?"

"Yes, we have had him to several specialists and each one is convinced that the boys problem is emotional not physical. We keep referring to him as a boy but he is a young man."

They sat around a table and each enjoyed a glass of wine. After a while Frank got up to leave explaining to the man that he had bought a cottage nearby and they would be seeing more of him.

He went to shake hands with Madame but he got a kiss on his cheeks, the man shook Frank's hand but Jacque insisted on giving Frank a hug.

The man who now introduced himself as Françoise, smiled; "You are the first stranger Jacque has accepted as a friend, I can only think something tragic happened to the boy in the past."

Frank went back to his cottage to finalize plans for when they return to the cottage as a family. Mary had offered to deal with all the new beds and bedding which they had previously selected and paid for but they would not be put into the cottage until the cats from the farmhouse had been roaming around inside the cottage for a couple of days. A cleaner has been engaged to clean right through the cottage after the cats had been removed.

Frank had found it to be a very tiring visit not just because of the hard physical work but he realized that if there were any problems crop up he would be dependent on Bob to deal with it. He made the arrangements to return home, which he enjoyed now driving held no fear to him.

*

Arriving home Frank received a great welcome from Beth, Lewis and Maisie, they all said how much they had missed him. Frank sat at the dinner table explaining all the work he had carried out and how he and Bob had found the bundles of money, they had taken it to the police station and were given a receipt, if it was not claimed in six months Bob and he could claim it. The money got the children really excited; Lewis decided he was going to take his magnetic gadget for looking for buried treasure. Looking at Lewis he said,"6,000 francs sounds a lot of money but when you work it out in Euro's, it will not amount to much working on the rate of exchange."

"I met a young man in the village, he is named Jacque, he is a wonderful boy but he is deaf and dumb. He is very badly disfigured; he has a deep scar going from his forehead round to the back of his head and he has the cheeks of his face torn, it has been said, it was caused by a bullet going through one cheek out through the other side.

When we go later in the year I want you to accept him as he is, please do not step back when he removes his baseball cap."

When the children had gone to bed and Frank was quite sure they couldn't hear their conversation. He then told Beth about the RAF tunics he found in the loft of the cottage and how the loft had been transformed into a living and sleeping room.

"The names and their service numbers were on tabs on the inside pockets of the tunics." He paused, "Beth, shall we just forget all about them or shall we try and trace what happened to these young men. I am very curious as whether they got home again, if so, would they like the tunics as a keepsake."

"Frank, just give the matter a lot of thought before you decide."

Chapter 4

Beth knew that Frank did not altogether agree with her, the more Frank thought about the tunics, the more he felt he should enquire if they were lucky enough to get back home after all the risks the resistance people had taken, in fact, some paid with their lives.

Frank contacted the local Air force Veterans Social group and requested to meet the Social Secretary.

Several days later he received a phone call from a Mr. John Dawes inviting him and his wife to the next monthly social meeting in a local hotel.

He told Beth the steps he had taken, she was not in the least surprised and she knew Frank was anxious to know what happened to the owners of the tunics.

Beth arranged with her mother to look after the children as she decided to go with Frank to meet the social secretary. Frank only took one tunic, that of Sergeant Worley.

When they arrived at the hotel John Dawes was waiting for them in the foyer, he took them into the bar area, bought drinks and they sat at a small table. Frank related all the details of how and where he had found the tunics, the more he told John the more excited he became.

"Frank. I will do my utmost to trace this young airman, what a story for him to tell his grandchildren." They sat talking for a while and Beth said she would have to go home and collect the children from her mother. They shook hands, "I will be in touch Frank."

*

Friday evening Beth picked up the children from their Friday nights activities, Masie from the Brownies and Lewis from the Cubs and they helped set the table ready for when their father came home from work, when he arrived home, Beth had the meal ready to put on the table. They had to listen, first to Maisie about what had taken place at the Brownies and what Brown Owl had to say, then Lewis told them about the rumour the other lads had got hold of, the scout leader was secretly meeting the

Brownies leader and they were both married. Beth just looked at Frank and smiled.

They had just finished their meal when the telephone started to ring; Frank lifted the receiver, before he could answer the caller said.

"May I speak to Frank Haines?"

"This is Frank Haines speaking, how can I help you?"

"My name is Gilbert Worley; I received news that you recovered my old RAF tunic from a French Cottage."

"That is right, I was curious to know if you did escape and get back home safely and if you would like your tunic as a keepsake?"

"Indeed I would, depending on what part of the country you are, I can visit anytime."

"I live in Marlow, do you know it?"

"Good lord, I live in Reading, it would be a very short journey. When will it be convenient for me to call? You said you were curious to know if I escaped, you will never believe the story I have to tell but true. I would suggest Sunday afternoon about 2 o'clock, if that would be convenient?"

"Great, I look forward to meeting you."

"Do you mind if we bring our grandchildren?"

"Not at all, my wife and I will be pleased to meet them."

Frank went back to the table; they all looked up expectantly, hoping he will fill in from the little of the conversation they heard. He looked across at Beth.

"Sergeant Worley is coming here Sunday afternoon at two o'clock, he appears anxious to retrieve his tunic." He looked at the children,

"I will explain what it is all about. When I was working in the loft of the French Cottage I found three RAF tunics, it was hearsay that the French resistance would hide any airman who had been shot down and help to get them back home. Having found the tunics it seems that there could be some credence to the rumours. He said that we will not believe the story of his escape."

After Sunday lunch they were all getting a little jumpy, wondering what they might expect from their visitors.

When they least expected it the doorbell rang, Frank went and opened the door, the man standing at the door was older than Frank had expected. The man smiled.

"Are you Frank Haines?"

"Yes, you must be Gilbert Worley, come in."

"May I bring my wife and grandchildren in with me?"

"You certainly can."

Beth rose from her chair and went outside to the car and when the lady wound down the window, Beth smiled.

"Do come inside, we have been looking forward to your visit."

When they all got inside the house Beth turned to her visitors.

"I am Beth and Frank you have met, smiling she said, these two urchins are Maisie and Lewis."

"This is Gilbert; I am Dulcie and these are Edna and Gordon "pointing to her grandchildren.

"Right, now we all know each other shall we have a cup of tea?"

"What a wonderful idea Beth."

The tea and cakes were placed on the table and the children soon made short work of cleaning the plates.

"Frank, before I get Dulcie to tell you the story of my escape and how I became a prisoner of war, will it upset your children at all? My family has heard the story many times and Dulcie will read it, I still find it too emotional to read and of course both my eyesight and memory is not as it used to be. It is a lifetime ago."

"Not at all Gilbert, you should see the frightening books they read."

Chapter 5

Gilbert Worley and his crew members were waiting for the transport to arrive and take them from their base to a dance, which, is being held at a nearby WAAF camp, they had all been invited.

When they entered the dance hall a big cheer went up from other members of their squadron. It was obvious that the bar had been kept very busy because some of the dancers began acting foolishly and a senior army officer stepped in and several were sent outside to cool off in the fresh air. As the evening progressed it did get a little noisy and Gilbert's squadron leader called them together and asked them to remain sober, in fact, he insisted.

He reminded them that they will be taking off on a flying mission early the following morning, the briefing had been held during the afternoon and he pointed out that he had stuck his neck out to allow them to attend the dance.

Any problems he will be held responsible and if he catches it in his neck, they will get it too.

The evening went very well apart from a few scuffles as one person tried to muscle in on another persons dance partner. On the whole, it was a very friendly evening.

There was quite a selection of the armed forces present; there were Army, Navy, Air force and Land Army girls. Quite a lot of the dancers were disappointed when it came time for the national anthem to be played. Gilbert and his crew members all dashed out to the waiting transport to take them back to base, arriving at the camp, they all went to their rooms and crawled into bed for about four hours sleep.

*

The crews were woken at 4.30 to get dressed into their fur lined leather jackets and boots. Food, coffee and tea was made available, some were joking and some were holding their heads but to say what little sleep they had, they all looked reasonably alert, they would object to the word but they will have to be alert as they are going to carry out a disciplined attack deep into the German countryside.

The crews boarded their Lancaster Bomber Aircraft, each hoping they will be back at this base in a few hours all in one piece; they have become hardened after seeing several of their friends blown out of the sky. It is only natural, the crews are a little fearful.

The navigator checked to ensure the Elsan Toilet had been cleaned and was on board, after last night; he thought it might become a necessity on this long trip.

They eased into their position inside the aircraft and Gilbert being the co-pilot sat beside the skipper, the blocks were taken away from the wheels by a member of the ground staff and Gilbert was instructed to start all four engines and taxi a little to a position in line with the other aircraft.

The aldis lamp flashed their plane number from the control tower, the pilot gave the engine full throttle and when they reached within a few hundred yards from the end of the runway, the pilot pulled the control stick operating the flaps, the plane started to rise.

The crew each started to exchange stories of the happenings at the dance the previous evening, you always find one clown in a group, the tail gunner started telling a lurid story about his dance partner and the skipper told him to shut up and test his guns before they leave the British coast.

Just before they reached the French coast they joined up with several other squadrons, Gilbert turned to the pilot.

"It's going to be a hum dinger tonight skipper."

"It certainly looks that way Gilbert."

They all listened to the steady hum of the engines, all surprised not to have come under attack, they expected a barrage from the ground as the Germans are now well bedded down in France. Just as they were thinking this, several enemy fighter aircraft were spotted above them preparing to attack, the senior officer in charge of the group alerted them to expect an attack.

Like a swarm of bees the Messerschmitt fighters came hurtling down, machine guns rattling away and one of Gilberts group was seen spiraling down on fire. When they broke off the attack the group leader told one badly damaged bomber to jettison his bombs and return to base, he will be met by fighter aircraft to protect him from enemy aircraft, he considered it wise for the plane to return to base to be repaired rather than lose another one of his aircraft.

It was a long trip and in spite of the warm clothing, all the crew began to bang their hands together to maintain circulation.

*

The crew heard instructions coming over their headphones, they were to be number five in the bombing run and every one must stay on their toes. The bomb aimer was in position and the navigator was working out the direction to give the skipper, when he asks the navigator after the bombing run.

"Where shall we go Bob?" Laughing as he will say it.

The gunners were scanning the skies for enemy aircraft. They could see a vast factory below them but the spot to bomb was indicated with flares which had been dropped by the Pathfinders Aircraft knowing other parts of the factory had been made to look like the vulnerable part.

The only voice to be heard was the bomb aimer asking the skipper to go left or a little right, then, Bombs gone. As the skipper was pulling the aircraft up, he shouted.

"Shall we go home Bob?"

The navigator gave the skipper the directions home amid loud nervous laughter and the skipper looked at his compass and smiled. The voice of the senior officer came into their headphones,

"Well done lads, right down their throat."

They travelled homeward bound for about half an hour, hoping to join up with the other planes in their squadron but it was upsetting to see gaps in the formations, indicating some had not survived anti aircraft guns or the German fighters.

It had become a joke among the crews, if it was their turn to pay for drinks and they were flying early the next day, they left the money behind the bar, just in case they did not return, sad but it became a tradition among some groups who treated it lightly but nevertheless, very sad.

Then, without expecting it, they came under heavy fire from the ground, all of a sudden there was a terrific explosion just below the aircraft and shrapnel penetrated the fuselage and ricocheted around the interior. Gilbert looked sideways and the skipper was covered with blood and it was painfully obvious he was dead.

He pushed the skipper to one side and took over the controls. He called the navigator over his intercom for help but he got no reply, he didn't get a reply from any member of the crew.

Two of the engines were not running and he noticed the remaining port engine was dripping fuel; he shut it down hoping to stop it catching fire. This left him with one starboard engine running but the plane was rapidly losing height and the one remaining engine started to falter, the shrapnel must have damaged all four engines.

He realized he would have to find an open space and put the plane down.

Gilbert felt he was so alone and faced with a very tricky situation, he must stay as calm as possible and try and save his own life.

Gilbert crash-landed the plane and lost consciousness for a while but he was not badly injured just cuts and bruises. When he came round, he was being dragged out of the blazing plane but being threatened with pitchforks and suddenly realized the men were speaking French.

He was carried over to a large farmhouse where he was cleaned up and his cuts and bruises attended to. He was given a hot drink and fainted again, when he came to, he found himself in different surroundings, it was a cottage.

He was given some food and a towel and shown into a small bathroom where he enjoyed a hot bath; he began to believe that he had died. He was given some old clothing so that he looked like a farm hand; they burned all of his clothes but he insisted on keeping his tunic for him to wear if he should get caught, otherwise he could be shot as a spy.

It was then he was guided into the loft, which, had been converted into living quarters.

"Still you know that Frank." The only time he was to open the trapdoor was if the small light bulb flashed three times and that was to receive food or a member of the resistance came to tell of any arrangements being made for him to be moved. The second day he was taken out of the loft and allowed to walk around for a while to exercise his legs, it was fantastic after being cooped up in the loft.

He lost count how many days he had been in the loft but after what seemed to be months, two young Frenchmen came one evening to take him to a small fishing village about three miles south of Calais, where he was to join a small fishing smack.

To get to the fishing village he travelled on a hay wagon, rode a bicycle and walked, it was a very tiring journey.

One of the young men was going with him, hoping to get to England; his family thought he would have a better chance than being transported to a labour camp.

Arriving at the fishing village he was put in a small safe house on the quayside and was to stay there until darkness, one of the boys said cheerio and the other boy stayed with him.

As the darkness crept in, two fishermen came for him and the young man, they were taken aboard the fishing boat, it was small and he was hoping they would not get any rough weather.

The darkness had now had completely closed in, the seamen prepared to set sail. He was told in the man's broken English.

"When we get about three miles out, we should see another boat signalling a code, you will transfer to that vessel to complete your journey."

He was given a glass of wine, which, they said they always do this when they set off to the fishing grounds.

Sailing along it was quite a pleasant evening and the sea was very calm, just as he had hoped for.

After a while one of the seaman said.

"There is a flashing light to the port bow, shall I steer towards it skipper?"

"Yes, it is using tonight's code."

They were steering towards the flashing light when a German E-Boat was seen speeding towards them and it came alongside; two German sailors jumped aboard the fishing boat and pulled the lever to stop the engine. They lined the four of us up and walked in front of us, one of them leaned forward and grabbed Gilberts service metal tag around his neck showing his rank and service number, using his automatic gun he pushed him to go aboard the E-Boat.

Then, they lined the skipper and his crew up and machine gunned them and as they were pulling away, they threw two hand grenades into the bilges of the fishing smack, when they exploded, it made a large hole in the bottom of the fishing boat and it sank. Gilbert was put ashore and taken to a Prisoners of War Camp. The villagers were devastated when the news filtered back to them, it was then they knew they must have a German mole in the village. The code used for the transfer of escapees is very secretly guarded by two people, the two captains and it is changed for each transfer.

He spent two years in a Prisoners of War Camp until the allied troops came to his rescue, not a very pleasant experience when he had almost made it back home two years earlier."

Nobody made a sound for a while; Frank looked up, "What a story, Gilbert" Lewis said,

"Where you frightened Mr. Worley?"

"Frightened Lewis, I was terrified, I was only a young man then."

"Did the young man wanting to get to England get shot?"

"Yes, the captain, a crew member and the young man were shot dead."

"In that case, you were very lucky to survive"

"I never thought I would live long enough to become an OAP but I have and I enjoy drawing my pension, each time I pick it up I count my blessings."

Beth made some more tea but they all decided to have something stronger and the toast was "Happy Days."

Frank got up out of his chair, he went to a cupboard and then handed Gilbert the tunic, as he took the tunic from Frank tears came into his eyes. He went to a tunic pocket and pulled out a crumpled photograph of Dulcie as a young girl.

"Thank you so much, I never thought I would see that again."

"You were so adamant that the tunic wasn't burned and yet you left it behind in the loft?"

"I had no option, the night I was taken to the fishing village was a sudden decision, in fact, all my flight records which, I treasured and all my belongings were left behind."

"Gilbert, now we have met, I would like to think we will keep in contact, you could always rent the cottage number four and we will be in number two, that number must be imprinted in your mind. I have not been altogether honest with you." Gilbert looked up suddenly.

"What haven't you told me?"

"There were three tunics, yours and two others, Flying Officer Hanlon and Pilot Officer Franks. I have not investigated the other two yet, I hesitated in your case, just in case I found something nasty had happened to you and this would have upset me. Now I have met you, I feel comfortable about tracing the other two. Can you recall meeting either of these two?"

"No, I did hear about their bravery but never had contact. If they are still alive, they too will probably be able to tell a hair-raising story similar to my own."

"I will ask the social secretary to check on the other two cases for me and I will contact you with the result."

*

Frank telephoned John Dawes and arranged to meet him. When they did meet Frank told him the story exactly as Gilbert had told him and his family. John was really upset when Frank told him Gilbert's story but delighted that Frank had been in touch with him.

Frank gave John the details from the other two tunics. John looked at Frank,

"I will do my best to trace these two officers."

The following day Beth told Frank, "I have received three telephone calls this afternoon from your customers. The first one was from Mrs. Arnold who want four interior doors replacing, the decorator has been ordered for next week, based on your promise that you would have completed the work this week-end.

The other two are smaller jobs, windows sticking, making it impossible to open, close and lock correctly." Frank realized he was neglecting his loyal customers: he would have to knuckle down and get his business up and running again and forget the Airmen's tunics for the time being

Chapter 6

Several days later, Frank received a phone call from John Dawes, telling him that he had traced Flying Officer Hanlon and would he and Beth meet him at the Social Club the following Thursday evening, Frank agreed. On arrival at the hotel John was waiting for them in the foyer accompanied by his wife, they went into the lounge where John introduced his wife Joyce to them.

Joyce turned to Beth saying, "John was so excited when Frank had told him you met Gilbert."

"Yes, when he told us his tale of trying to return to this country, it brought tears to my eyes."

*

John came back from the bar with the drinks; he sat down and said "I have now traced Pilot Officer Hanlon to the RAF hospital in Walters Ash, which, as you know is just the other side of High Wycombe, about half an hours drive from where you live."

"The other night I attended a group meeting and I told them Gilbert's story, they couldn't believe such a thing could happen, of course, they have never served in the forces. Several remarked, what! A film that would make," another member said.

"That is the story we know about but how many sad stories we have not heard and never will hear."

"Stephen is in a wheelchair paralyzed from the hip down, when he first arrived back in this country he was taken to Stoke Mandeville near Princes Risborough where they specialize in back injuries but they could do little to help him.

His wife has moved home from Manchester to live near the camp to enable her to visit regularly; the RAF association helped her to make the move and to obtain suitable part-time employment, thus enabling her to remain independent. I do not know if he was injured trying to escape or since his return home."

Beth looked across at Frank.

"Oh! No, Frank."

"Beth, the hospital is only about ten minutes from where your sister lives in Naphill."

"Don't you two start arguing, I will have to be the referee" said John laughing.

"Was Gilbert pleased to get his tunic back?" Joyce asked.

"Yes, His eyes filled with tears when Frank handed it to him."

*

They sat having breakfast on the Saturday morning, Beth looked across at Frank.

"Frank, ring the RAF Hospital at Walters Ash and enquire if Stephen Hanlon is still a patient there, if so, is it convenient to visit tomorrow afternoon. I have checked and I think it will be a 45 minute drive?" Frank smiled.

He rang the hospital number John had given him; the nurse who answered the phone said, "Stephen is still a patient here and you can visit Sunday afternoon anytime, we do not restrict visiting hours."

The children decided to remain at home with their grandparents, secretly their parents were pleased the children had made that decision.

At the top of Marlow Hill, Frank pointed across the town of High Wycombe to the other side of the valley, saying.

"Walters Ash is just on the other hillside."

Arriving at the camp's car park, they were given instruction how to get into the hospital.

They entered the main door and approached the reception desk; a young lady came to them wearing a broad smile asking the name of the person they were visiting.

"What a change to be greeted in this manner," said Frank.

She guided them into a lounge area and asked if they would like coffee or tea, they both asked for tea. When she got them settled with their tea and biscuits she excused herself and left the room.

They heard chatter and laughter coming from the corridor and the young lady came into the room pushing a man in a wheelchair. Frank was really surprised to see Stephen, he was quite elderly. Frank frequently forgets how the years have gone by since the war ended. "This is Stephen

Hanlon and believe me he gives us a lot of trouble," she burst out laughing.

Frank stood up, "I am Frank Haines and this is my wife Beth and we are pleased to meet you."

"My name, as you know is Stephen Hanlon and I am wheelchair bound but that is another story. I am delighted that you have come to visit me but I am a little puzzled, why are you here? Have we met before or are you a member of a group who visits hospitals?"

Frank smiled.

"I will tell you why we are here. We recently bought an old dilapidated cottage in a French village, when I was in the process of renovating, hoping to make it habitable again, bearing in mind the cottage had been boarded up for many years, 5 years that we know of. While I was working in the loft area, I found three Air force tunics, one of them had your name, service number and rank on the inside pocket.

I brought them back home with me hoping to trace their owners. I have already traced one; it belonged to Sgt Pilot Gilbert Worley, he did not know the owners of the other two tunics. He told us a terrific story of his effort to escape, which, turned out to be unsuccessful but the look on his face when I handed him his old tunic was incredible, it still contained a photograph of his girlfriend, now his wife. Obviously, you will remember the cottage to which I am referring. There have been many rumours circulating what happened to the owners.

When we bought the cottage there were still dirty plates and cutlery on the table, in fact, there was great difficulty in finding the owners to complete the purchase, which turned out to be the descendants of the farm owner."

"I do hope that the elderly couple did not come to any harm, they were or still are wonderful people, thinking about it, if they are still alive they must be nearly 100 years old. At one time, the man was beaten up just as a warning, for what? The villagers were very upset that this should happen and it was discovered later, the gang of thugs who had beaten him so badly were Frenchmen, members of the Vichy Malice Group."

"During my convalescence in York, the Matron was very concerned about the state of mind of many of her residents and she was a very clever lady. She came up with an idea which made all the residents come to life and all talking and joking."

After dinner one evening, she called her family together; she referred to the residents as her family.

"I want you all to write about a particular time you served in the forces and when you have all finished and handed the article in to me, I will read one or two each evening after dinner. When I have read them all out I will give you a slip of paper and we will have a secret ballot on which article you think was the better one, no one will know the name of the author until after you have voted."

"No expense has been spared and the winner will be presented with a BAR OF CHOCOLATE."

"Oddly enough it was a tie, three winners and it was a hilarious ceremony held to share the bar of chocolate into three pieces exactly. You will never understand the fun we had that evening. There were claims that the voting had been rigged but every one got a slice of chocolate a very clever move on the part of the matron; every one was discussing their experiences and each one trying to outdo his neighbour for days on end. The nurse has a copy of my story and I am sure she will read it out for you."

"Stephen, I will read it out with pleasure; it is wonderful, so humane."

Frank said, "We will be delighted to listen."

Stephen and his wife Vera were sat down having breakfast together; it was the first time for many days as his flying duties have taken over his life due to the enemy air attacks. This is causing a little friction in their household, Vera complains that they never go out together or attend the dance at the base, which is held three times each week. He could not take Vera out as much as he would like due to the pressure of flying duties. The camp commander realized they were asking a lot from their fighter squadrons but they are so desperate for pilots and aircraft to protect the bombers from enemy fighters.

*

A full scale offensive was being carried out on the enemy's large engineering factories and train depots to hinder the movement of troops. Stephen's squadron duties were to protect the bombers setting out on a daylight raid; he had been airborne for twenty minutes when the engine of his Hurricane started to misfire, he radioed the base and was ordered to return to the base. When he landed he handed his plane over to the flight engineer.

He reported to the camp commander who told him to report back at 1800 hours to carry out a patrol over the South Coast. He jumped into his MG sports car and drove home.

He was a little surprised when he couldn't find Vera but when he went upstairs to change his clothes; there was Vera in bed with another man. Stephen was so angry; he had come home early to find his wife in bed with another man, his whole world collapsed.

Should he physically attack them both, shout loudly or just order them both out of the house.

The tunic on the bedroom chair had pips on the shoulder epaulettes indicating that the man in bed with his wife is an army officer.

*

He went downstairs, opened the French windows and walked out into the garden and he was violently sick. Vera walked out of the house to him.

"Stephen, I am so sorry, this is the first time anything like this has happened."

"Do you expect me to believe that Vera, what you mean, it is the first time I have come home early and you have been caught out?"

Vera burst into tears. "Please forgive me Stephen."

He looked at her.

"Pack your bags and go and stay with your parents, we will sell our house in Windsor, clear the mortgage and share the remaining money between us."

"Please don't do this Stephen,"

Before he could answer the phone rang, he picked up the receiver, and listened to the caller. "Is my plane ready? I will be there in 10 minutes," he picked up his bag, went outside, jumped into his car and drove back to the base.

When he arrived, it was a hive of activity and he could see his plane was on the apron ready for him. A meeting was quickly called; intelligence reports are that eighty enemy aircraft are approaching the south coast.

We are not sure of their target, they are playing games. Stephen joined his squadron leader and other fighter pilots in the conference room. The officer was standing on a platform at the front of the room and was pointing to a large screen, indicating the direction of the incoming enemy aircraft. The strategy to be adopted was explained and instructed which squadron covers which area.

Stephen sat in his Hurricane waiting to be given the signal to take off; he was to fly in a formation of three planes. The enemy aircraft were spotted crossing the cliffs of Dover; the Hurricanes immediately increased their height to give them the advantage of speed in attack. They plummeted down to attack the bombers, Stephen had one of the aircraft in his gun sight, he fired, the plane appeared to halt in its flight, turned and spiraled out of control enveloped in flames. Stephen was excited but at the same time a little sad, he is responsible for the death of a family member. Bullets started hitting his plane, he felt a searing pain in his right shoulder, he quickly twisted and turned and he got on the tail of a Dornier aircraft, he fired his guns and again the plane appeared to halt in flight and then went down with a trail of smoke.

His squadron leader called over the radio ordering them back in formation and to return to base due to their low fuel tanks. The pilots all sat down on the chairs for the debriefing.

They were surprised how many enemy aircraft they had destroyed between them. Stephen went to get out of his chair and collapsed, the shoulder of his flying suit was sodden with blood. He was taken by ambulance to a nearby hospital as the sick bay at the base was completely full.

The surgeons operated to repair the shattered shoulder bones and stitched the flesh wounds; he was sedated and allowed to rest for a few days.

When they told him that he was going back to the sick bay at the base, he was delighted. Two days after his return, Vera came to visit, his manner towards Vera was very cool but gradually he mellowed. During Vera's visit the Senior Medical Officer came to Stephen's bedside saying, "Sorry Stephen you will have to go back to the hospital we are expecting a large number of injured crew members during the today's raid."

Looking at Vera he said, "This man needs looking after and plenty of rest."

Vera smiled,

"Couldn't I take him home to look after him but your medical staff will have to visit and change his dressings. That would take some of the pressure off your staff."

"That would be great help if you think you could manage it," laughing as he said it. Vera looked at Stephen first then the Medical Officer,

"I'm sure there will no problem, I will go home now and make preparations for him to return home, will you arrange transport to bring him home, give me a couple of hours."

"Sorry Vera, it will be in one hour, the planes are due back in about one and a half hours with many casualties and I am not sure of the transport situation, I will ring you." Vera felt very sorry for the families who will be receiving a telegram from the Air Ministry, telling them that their loved ones are either dead or badly injured.

Vera arrived home and immediately went upstairs to make a bed ready for when Stephen is brought home. She prepared the bed in the smaller room; this room has an en suite and according to the M.O. Stephen's medication will make him visit the toilet more often than normal.

*

The ambulance arrived and the medical staff insisted on helping him upstairs to his bedroom. He felt a bit of a fraud as he only had a damaged shoulder but it was in a heavy plaster caste.

Vera got him settled in bed and she fussed around and really looked after him, whatever he wanted she was there to deal with it.

Stephen realized the way Vera was caring for him, made him wonder if he had gone off the handle in the wrong way. What Vera did was totally wrong but thinking back, he remembered that he had cheated on Vera on more than one occasion but he was never caught or found out. When Vera came into the room carrying a tray of food, he said.

"Put the tray down and come here."

She hesitated but he reached out and put his good arm round her shoulders, she looked at him, "Am I forgiven?"

He didn't answer but he gently kissed her on her lips.

"Yes Vera, I couldn't live without you." Vera burst into tears.

Stephen's health progressed rapidly and after three months he was passed medically fit to fly, much to the base commander's relief as he was still under pressure. Stephen did several patrols over the south coast without encountering any enemy aircraft.

All the fighter pilots were called into the conference room and told they will be protecting several squadrons of bombers going deep into Germany.

"Before I get questioned, your aircraft will be fitted with auxiliary fuel tanks, which, can be jettisoned when empty and your engines will be automatically connected to your normal fuel tanks, this give you longer flying hours. The clever boys have spent months working on this project and it has been tested on numerous occasions. Gentlemen, you can feel comfortable with the new arrangement."

*

The squadron of fighter aircraft took off and met up with the bombing squadrons over the English Channel, they were travelling across France. Suddenly their squadron leader shouted into the phone, good lord. There are enemy fighters above us, he hadn't got the words out when dozens of enemy fighter aircraft came hurtling out of the skies and Stephen was one the first to be hit and he saw pieces of his plane falling. Vera became very worried as she did not get her usual telephone call from Stephen on his return from flying. The following morning, she heard a knock on the front door, when she opened the door she was handed the dreaded telegram.

Her hands were trembling so bad she had difficulty in opening the envelope. She read as far as, the Air Ministry regrets, she felt unable to read any more but she steeled herself and read he was missing. Vera was dreadfully upset and she sat crying. The telephone rang, she said hello in a faltering voice.

"Hello Vera, this is Ralph, I'm ringing to put your mind at rest. I saw Stephen parachute out of his Hurricane I circled to prevent any enemy pilot doing anything silly, he landed and waved, I dipped my wing in acknowledgement, let us hope the resistance group finds him before the Germans."

"Thank you Ralph, I am so pleased he landed safely and thank you for finding the time to ring me."

He had parachuted out of his Hurricane fighter when a Messerschmitt fighter had shot his tail off; when he landed he was immediately picked up and he thought they were Germans. He was taken to the cottage, the injuries to his head were cleaned and a plaster stuck on to keep it clean. It was only then, he realized they belonged to the French Resistance party. After being fed he was put in the loft, which was very comfortable.

Several days later he had a visit from one of the leaders of the resistance group, he came to tell him that plans had been made to take him close to the Swiss border; from where he should be able to get back to England. The plan was, he would be placed in an empty wine barrel, and (he was to go downstairs later that evening to make sure he can fit in the barrel). He will be travelling on a wagon containing twenty barrels of wine to be delivered to a German warehouse near the Swiss border.

Two nights later he was taken from the cottage and handed over to two men dressed as draymen wearing long leather aprons. He was then taken into a barn where he met a Polish airman who had been shot down while operating from an English airfield. They were each placed in an empty wine barrel and it was uncomfortable especially when he felt the barrel being lifted, jarred and rolled into position on the flat topped wagon.

He had been told the journey would take five to six hours but it seemed forever, his limbs felt that they no longer belonged to him.

The engine stopped and he could hear a lot of shouting and barrels being moved and then he heard the man in charge telling his men to put the empty barrels they had on the wagon. The engine started up and he heaved a sigh of relief but suddenly the Polish pilot started to sing at the top of his voice, realizing the problem the driver put his foot down on the accelerator and sped off in the direction of Switzerland.

*

When I told the story to the men who carried out my debriefing, they were convinced that the Polish man had been intoxicated, breathing in the fumes from the used Wine barrel.

The driver shouted telling them to try and get out of the barrel, he heard machine gunfire and the next thing he was conscious of was the wagon rolling over down a very steep hill. When the wagon came to a halt, there was more gunfire and then it went deathly quiet.

He was underneath several barrels of wine and could hardly move but eventually he did manage to crawl out from underneath.

He went to stand up and he just collapsed, he could not walk. As he lay on the ground he could see the border sentry a few hundred yards ahead, he rolled over on to his belly and propelled himself along using his elbows. By the time he got to the border the skin on his arms and elbows were hanging off in strips and bleeding, the guard dragged him over the Swiss border and called for an ambulance. He was taken to the local hospital and the Red Cross took care of him and arranged for his repatriation.

*

Arriving home, he was taken to Stoke Mandeville where he stayed for several months, from there he was taken to several different hospitals, hoping they could repair his broken back but as you can see, they were unsuccessful." Beth sat listening with tears running down her cheeks. The nurse folded the sheet of paper and handed it to Stephen.

Frank stood up, "Excuse me; while I go to my car, I shouldn't be many minutes."

He returned with a parcel under his arm.

"Here is your old tunic; I thought you might like it as a keepsake."

"Wonderful Frank, thank you. When you go back to the cottage just enquire if any of the villagers of that time are still around and alive, thank them for me."

On the way home Beth turned to Frank,

"I hope we will not have to sit and listen to another sad story about the third tunic you discovered at our cottage. I find the stories very distressing."

"Beth, I was quite young when all these atrocities were taking place, one cannot believe a few could treat mankind in such a way. As they got older they must had great difficulty with living with themselves after treating people in such a manner and these experiences we are listening to took place several years ago."

Several days later John Dawes telephoned Frank and told him.

"The Air Ministry can't find Pilot Officer Franks in any of the war time records and even his service number is not recorded. Have they been removed for some reason, if so, by whom? There appears to be so many anomalies surrounding this airman, I can't give you much hope in finding him, I suggest you keep the tunic and hope your quest will arrive at a satisfactory conclusion sometime in the future. No airman, no escape story."

*

The following day, Mrs. Dawes had two visitors asking to speak to her husband John, she told them he would be home this evening if they would care to call later. When John arrived home, his wife, Joyce, told him to expect a visitor sometime in the evening. As expected, at seven o'clock the door bell rang. When he opened the door he found two gentlemen on the doorstep. One man asked. "May we come inside and speak to you?"

John stepped to one side to allow them to enter.

"Mr. Dawes. The Air Ministry has advised us that you have been making enquiries about Pilot Officer Lance Franks. Why? Do you have any reason you want to trace him?"

John explained that his friend Frank had found three tunics in an old French Cottage, we have traced two who are now elderly and returned the tunics to them, with which, they were delighted, they never thought they would ever see them again.

"My friend Frank Haines bought an old dilapidated French cottage, it was rumoured that this cottage had been used by the French resistance during the German, occupation.

When Frank started to work on the cottage hoping to make it habitable again he found three RAF tunics in the loft, they were in a disgusting state as they had been lying in a corner of the loft for forty years. Frank got the tunics cleaned up and we managed to trace two of the personnel and believe me they were delighted to have them once again, one still had a photograph of his girlfriend in one pocket and now is his wife.

One was Sergeant Worley and the other was John Hanlon. The stories they told about the attempted escape are well worth listening to. Incidentally, John Hanlon is in a wheel chair permanently, he was badly injured while trying to escape, in fact, his broken back is the reason he spends a lot of time in Walters Ash, R.A.F. Hospital. He can do nothing for himself and is entirely dependant on help from the nursing staff and now he is quite elderly."

*

Frank was very surprised when the two MI5 gents called at his house asking him about the tunics. "We understand from John Dawes you have traced two of the airman and returned their tunics to them but not the third one, named Lance Franks."

"That is correct"

"May I see his tunic?"

Frank went to a cupboard, took it down from the hangar and handed it to the MI5 agent.

The agent then produced a legal looking document. "This paper allows me to commandeer the tunic."

Frank starred at the agent, "Look here, why do you want the tunic?"

"The Air Ministry has demanded its return."

With that answer, he put the tunic over his arm and put his hand out to shake hands with Frank. As they drove off in a RAF car, Frank stood with his mouth open in surprise. There must be some escape story there to be told but no one is going to hear it.

Chapter 7

Pilot Officer Lance Frank's Wellington bomber was badly damaged by gunfire while on a bombing run over a German engineering factory; he managed to maintain sufficient height to enable his crew to parachute from the aircraft before he crash-landed. The plane had been flying for several hours to arrive at the target and they were all disappointed that the plane was so badly damaged before they had time to drop all of their bombs on the target instead of being jettisoned. Lance had great difficulty in holding the plane steady, he was hoping to get half way over the English Channel before ditching and then, he stood a good chance of being picked up by the Air Sea Rescue operating with MTB fast craft. Suddenly he lost all power and he wrestled with the controls hoping to crash-land the plane the right way up and have a chance to survive. When he did land he lost consciousness. When he came round he found himself being pulled out of his burning bomber by some French farm workers and taken to a farmhouse where a doctor from the village tended his broken arm and burns.

After treatment he was taken to a local village cottage and put into a loft area where he spent several months recovering. He was very well fed and cared for; he realized he was fortunate to be among such good friends but had difficulty to remain reasonably sane, just sat in the loft. Several evenings one of the farmer's daughters named Anna, would come into the loft, sit with him and talk. Lance began to really look forward to her visits and gradually they became very close and Anna was very upset when Lance was moved away. The local people wanted to hear all the news of what was happening in Britain and how the people were standing up to the German bombing and they were very encouraged with his reply.

Lance laid back wondering if he is lucky or unlucky, his mind wandered back over the years. When he was a small child travelling in a car with both his parents and they were involved in a car crash, he can vaguely remember his parents being taken away in an ambulance and he was taken to a relative's home. His aunty was very kind to him and it was she, who told him both of his parents had been killed but Uncle Ted was a big bully and no time for anyone except Ted. Lance lived with them until he was eight years old, then friends of his father arranged for him to be sent to a Masonic boarding school, they paid all the costs and arranged for Lance to receive a monthly income, one day he plans to find them and thank them for giving him such a good start. Lance did very well and he achieved a scholarship into a university, where again, he did exceptionally well. The subject he excelled in was languages; he had such an aptitude for picking up a language that his tutors encouraged him to make this his major. He joined the Civil Service with a view to becoming an interpreter but the secret service seniors moved him to the intelligence offices of the service. Lance was gradually groomed to become a spy and that was to be his career but the war intervened and he was seconded into the R. A. F. he was to snoop around to ensure there were no nests of German spies or 5th column activities that Mr. Winston Churchill was always warning about. The country became so short of pilots, Lance was trained as bomber pilot. He pondered; I wonder who will receive the telegram telling them he is missing

*

One evening he was told that arrangements were being made to move him to another safe house nearer the coast; he was fitted out in a farm labourers outfit.

That evening he was taken from the cottage under the cover of darkness, hidden under a pile of straw on a hay wagon. They had only travelled one mile from the cottage when they were stopped and arrested by well-armed soldiers but it turned out they were Russians, not Germans.

Lance Franks was separated from the resistance group who were surprisingly allowed to return home and he was taken to a prison cell in the Russian sector, which was shocking. It had no washing or toilet facilities and it was freezing cold.

Several hours later the cell door was unlocked and a soldier entered carrying a plate of food and a cup of coffee, the cup was filthy. A Russian Army Officer followed the soldier into the cell, he nodded to the soldier to leave and he sat and watched Lance eat the food, Lance was a little hesitate about drinking from the dirty mug but he was so thirsty, he did.

The Russian sat, not speaking just staring and watching Lance.

*

When Lance had finished eating, the Russian smiled at him and spoke to him using the Russian language, Lance responded, the officer smiled again.

"Good, I thought we had captured the right man. You were trained as a British spy leading up to when you were enlisted into the British Air Force. My information is, that you are a linguist and you speak English, which is your native tongue, Russian, French, German and Spanish, is that correct comrade?"

"Yes, that is correct but why are you interested in me?"

"I am hoping you and I can go into business together, what you British refer to as forming a company."

"Whatever you are talking about I am not interested."

*

"Okay, we will discuss it again tomorrow." Turning round he walked out of the cell, locking the cell door behind him.

Lance spent an uncomfortable night, he was very cold and badly bitten by the bugs in the dirty palliasse and he began to think perhaps he should listen to the Russian's proposition.

Lance sat on the edge of his bunk wondering what the day will bring, he was still pondering when or what the Russian finds Lance useful to him.

The cell door opened and the soldier standing outside the cell beckoned Lance to follow him. Lance came out of the cell and followed the soldier up a flight of stairs into a large room which looked like a kitchen, the soldier pointed to a door on the right hand side of the corridor, he entered the room and the door was closed behind him.

He looked around and saw the Russian officer sat at a small table covered with a spotlessly clean white tablecloth, the officer looked up.

"Good morning, come and sit down, would you like an English breakfast?"

Lance was served with two rashers of bacon, two sausages, fried bread and two eggs, he was given the choice of tea or coffee and he really enjoyed the meal.

He turned to the Russian officer.

"What have you in mind?"

"Lance, it is Lance, yes?"

"Yes that is my name, what shall I call you?"

"Just call me Ivan, which, seems to be the name how the Europeans refer to us. Now Lance, I will explain to you what I have in mind.

Governments pay handsomely for any international secrets and that is why they train so many agents. We will set up a worldwide company buying secrets from international spies and sell the secrets to the country being threatened or to the highest bidder?"

"How would you finance such an undertaking?"

"With Gold."

"Gold?"

"Yes, I have 50 bars of gold hidden"

"I am hoping when we return to France, using your rank and with a little bribery you can borrow an RAF truck for a few hours to move the gold. You can bribe the sergeant or who is in charge of the transport pool with a quarter of a gold bar, which should command a good price, especially as the war is just about over. The currency markets will be all cockeyed for a year or so after the war has finished and gold will be the thing to have."

"I wasn't aware I had left France Ivan."

"You were sedated when we captured you and now you are in Germany, which lessens the chance of you doing a runner. We need a truck large enough to transport my crate of gold bars to a building, which, I have rented near Potsdam and it is there we will make our headquarters. I have made arrangements to have the very latest communication and security equipment installed.

Germany is being carved up, making Berlin in four sections the allies each being responsible for a sector and each will be looking over their shoulders to see what the other countries are up to and they are all very suspicious of each other. There is a fortune to be made buying and selling secrets and I intend to cash in and I would like you to join me. If however, you decide against joining me, I trust you not to discuss my plans with any other person but I think you will enjoy the challenge."

Lance asked Ivan to allow him a few hours to consider his offer.

Later that day Ivan called to see Lance.

"Have you decided yet?"

"Yes Ivan, I have decided to join your venture."

"Lance, we must set up your name and your background, we must be very careful to leave no gaps and make it a solid story. If the KGB discovers the slightest chink in your story, they will dig and dig until they arrive at the truth and if they consider you a threat, they will destroy you. I suggest you rent a room in the American sector until our flats are ready in Potsdam.

We will have to collect the gold, from where, I do not know, it was in France but one crate disappeared during a break-in and the people entrusted with its safe Keeping, are moving the gold to a safer place. Bearing in mind there are forty crates to move so it will be a mammoth task. We should be able to collect the gold and transport it without much trouble, quite a few officers have got their share and I don't mean just Russian Officers."

Lance found the nearest RAF station to Potsdam and decided to visit. When he visited the reception area he found the staff to be most hostile, he decided not to approach them regarding the truck. Lance wandered into the Officers mess and ordered a cup of coffee, he sat drinking his coffee and enjoying a cigar, which, was one of Lance's vices. A voice said.

"May I join you?"

"Certainly, I will be glad of some company."

"My name is Harry, what are your duties now?"

"My name is Lance." He stood up and shook Harry by the hand.

"I shall be returning to England shortly, I have been held as a prisoner of war for a year or so. I was shot down while operating in a bombing raid over Germany and now I am free." (At this stage, he thought it better not to mention the cottage or the name of the village.)

"What are duties here or are you going home?"

"No, I am in charge of the transport depot here; my main problem is safeguarding the fuel, which, if stolen, would be sold on the black market." Lance turned to Harry.

"I went to your office this morning, hoping I could hire a truck but the staff was so off hand I decided against it."

"Is it just a small truck?"

"Yes, it is to help a friend of mine to move furniture back to his house, it had been hidden to prevent it being destroyed or stolen. He is prepared to pay for the hire of the truck with gold."

"How much gold are we talking?"

"A quarter of a gold bar, in fact, if you are willing to help, I will enquire the exact weight you would receive and its value."

"Meet me here tomorrow with that information and if I think it is a fair deal we will be in business. Lance we must keep our transaction very quiet, what I am doing is no worse than the corruption that is going on but I would hate to be the one caught out."

They sat drinking their coffee discussing their home life and families and what their hopes are for the future. Harry stood up offering his hand to Lance;

"We will meet for coffee tomorrow morning, okay?"

When Lance met up with Ivan, he was surprised; Ivan did not appear his usual self-assured person. Lance explained how he had met Harry and he felt sure he would come across with a truck.

"Lance, if Harry is agreeable I will give him half a gold bar. The dealers appear to be reluctant to buy gold at present, all they are interested in buying is American Dollars that is the reason I am increasing my offer, based on the difficulty and the time involved to find a market paying a reasonable price."

Lance met Harry as planned and told him that Ivan will increase his offer to half a gold bar in view of the difficulties to sell gold at the moment in time. The value of gold is fluctuating hourly.

"Lance, the Russians have flooded the market with Reich marks making them worthless and the Allies have introduced Deutsche marks, which, are not regarded as legal tender by the Russians in many parts of Germany, particularly in Berlin. The Russians are still trying to keep Germany weak. No, if I get you a truck I will expect 100 American Dollars.

That is my offer Lance, check with your friend and advise if I am to go ahead?"

"Harry, I will personally guarantee that you will get the fee you are asking for the hire of the truck. I will meet you tomorrow to make the final arrangements."

"No better still Lance, if I bring the truck here you will be able to move the furniture and return the truck here; in fact, I will drive the truck for you, if you wish?"

"That is a good idea but I will have to check with my friend."

Lance telephoned Ivan but he didn't agree, he would rather drive and deal with the transfer of the gold himself. His main concern is, the number of Russian soldiers roaming around, which, could cause problems but he was sure he could deal with them.

*

Two days later Lance and Ivan joined Harry for coffee; it was arranged that they will take the truck that is parked outside the café bar in the car park and return the vehicle at six o'clock. Harry handed Ivan the ignition keys, when Ivan got into the drivers seat he was a little uncertain with the controls but he soon became acclimatized with them, Lance got in and they drove off. They had been travelling for about one hour when Ivan pulled into a long driveway leading to a small house with a large barn beside it.

"You stay here Lance, I will go into the barn and make myself known, if however, I encounter any language problems I will call you." Which, he did. There were several high ranking officers in the barn, all different nationalities. Ivan's crate was pointed out to him, he was handed a small crowbar and he levered open the top of the crate, he then counted the gold bars and found he had 50 bars which, was his share. He reversed the truck into the barn and the crate was loaded on to the truck using a forklift. Lance just smiled.

"We will have to unload by carrying one at a time."

Ivan just raised his eyebrows and got back into the driving seat. He waved farewell to the Army Officers who were standing around the door of the barn.

"They wanted me to leave you here Lance; they are experiencing great difficulties with the various languages being used when people arrive to collect their share. I had to pull rank to bring you away."

"Ivan, you told me that we would have a long journey to France to collect the gold and yet we have only travelled one and quarter hours, how come?"

"The crates were moved because of a break in to the premises where the crates were stored; they arrived here two days ago. You must admit, it is more convenient for us to collect."

"Right Lance, Potsdam is our next destination."

Lance was very surprised when they arrived at the building Ivan had rented, with an opportunity to buy at a later date. The building was constructed with stone blocks and bricks, all the windows were protected with heavy metal grills. The door was made of steel with a heavy steel grill, in fact, the building looks impregnable. Ivan opened the grill but when he opened the steel door, a high pitched siren sounded until he switched the alarm off with a key.

When Lance entered the large office he was astounded with the layout.

The room had three telephones and four radio communication consoles. Ivan walked to the corner of the room and opened a hinged part of the wall which exposed a large steel safe.

"Lance let us unload the truck and put the gold in the safe for now. I hope we can prosper from the venture, apart from the profit, I am sure we will enjoy ourselves."

After unloading the gold and putting it in the safe, they set off to return the truck to Harry. Ivan had the 100 US dollars in an envelope as promised. Harry walked into the café, looking round he spotted Lance and Ivan; he bought a drink and joined them at their table. Ivan passed the envelope under the table.

"Don't count it here Harry; there is 100 US Dollars in the envelope as we agreed."

"Very good, the truck is outside, I saw it as I came in. Have you got the keys or have you left them on the dashboard?"

Ivan passed the ignition keys to Harry; he stood up shaking hands with Ivan and Lance then he left.

Chapter 8

Ivan called Lance. "We have received our first call; it is from a man calling himself Grumpy. He claims to have information about the execution of an American Army Officer named Captain Carter. The reason for this planned execution is because when he and his troops entered a small village, he allowed them to rape, steal and humiliate the villagers, this has been planned for a long time. To advise when, where and how the execution will take place will cost 600 American dollars. I have a telephone number to contact Grumpy after we have spoken to the American authorities.

Incidentally, Captain Carter is the son of an American Senator, surely they will want to prevent this happening; in this case money must be of the secondary importance. As it is a message dealing with an American, I would prefer you to contact them."

Lance made a few phone calls and eventually found the phone number of Brigadier General Brook, the man in charge of the American sector in Berlin. Lance telephoned the number and asked to speak to the Brigadier but was told by the switchboard operator that he would be put through to one of the Brigadiers' aides. After ringing out for a while a man answered the phone. "This is Colonel Clarke, can I help you?"

"Yes, this is Pilot Officer Franks.

We have been approached by an international spy who is offering you information to prevent the execution of American Army Officer Carter. The execution is being planned by a village, in which, this officer allowed his men to rape, steal and humiliate the occupants of this village. To provide you with the information of where, when and how the execution is planned will cost 1200 US dollars. Colonel, I can personally assure you it isn't a hoax, we've had dealings with this man before. It seems to be a small price to save a man's life. One other thing you should know, this Officer is the son of one of your Senators."

"Hang on, I will have a word with the Brigadier, it is he who make the decisions." Lance just sat waiting for the colonel to return. He heard the phone being picked up.

"Hi, the Brigadier is refusing to pay money out on a hoax phone call."

"It is not a hoax Colonel; I will ring you back in about twenty minutes to allow him further thoughts."

"I don't think he will change his mind."

Lance rang the number later asking to speak to Colonel Clarke.

"Hello, sorry the Brigadier will not entertain a hoax call, he is not convinced it is a true account."

*

Several days later, Lance heard that Captain Carter had been killed the previous night but no information was available of how the captain had died.

Lance was convinced that Ivan had a hand in the Captains death.

Later that day, Lance was in the communication room when Ivan walked in, it was obvious to Ivan that Lance was upset about something.

"What is wrong?"

"When I joined you in this venture, I thought I was joining an honourable man, not a man who would kill."

"What on earth are you talking about Lance?"

"Captain Carter was killed last night."

"Surely you don't think that I had anything to do with his death?" Ivan walked out of the room.

Twenty minutes later Ivan came back into the room carrying two cups of coffee. He walked up to Lance and handed him a cup of coffee.

"I have just made a phone call and have been told that Captain Carter walked out of a bar last night the worst for wear. He was so drunk that he had great difficulty getting into his jeep; in fact, he was so drunk he shouldn't have driven.

However, he drove off heading for the barracks, he was driving too fast and when he came to a very sharp bend he lost control and he veered on the wrong side of the road and collided head on with an army tank that was out on night manoeuvres, he was killed instantly."

"Ivan, I owe you an apology to even think you would ever consider such an act."

"Think nothing of it Lance but it could make people sit up and realize that we don't tell fairy stories. At least the villagers weren't responsible, or were they, I wonder?"

Lance went off to bed and Ivan just sat thinking over the happenings over the past few days. He was shaken out of his reverie, one of the phones started to ring. Ivan picked up the phone.

"My name is Rook that is my chosen name for such transactions. I have some information which I will sell for 600US dollars."

"What or whom does your information refer to?"

"The information, is regarding a problem in the Russian sector of Berlin."

"Yes, we are very interested in buying but will you ring back in 15 minutes and the man dealing with that area will take your call."

Ivan thought, he being a Russian he should leave well alone.

The phone started to ring and this time Lance picked up the receiver, before he could speak a voice said,

"I was told to ring back in 15minutes."

"Hello, are you Rook?"

"Yes, that is my name. I have some information for sale, it is regarding the Russians dismantling an engineering factory during the hours of darkness and the factory is surrounded by their army, like a ring of steel to keep out any one other than the workers.

This is one of the factories that produced the V2 rocket, used to bombard England at the latter part of the war. The Russians are desperate to discover the secrets of the engine propulsion system and the rocket construction; in fact, they want to know everything about it because they considered it was before its time. I have all the information when all this is to take place and how it is going to be transported to an airfield and loaded on one of their larger aircraft bound for Russia. The one problem they are facing is how to install the lifting gear at the airfield, to lift the machinery from the flat topped wagons and then transfer on to flat 10 wheeled trolley to wheel on to the plane. They are discussing the use of slave German labour to erect the lifting gear at the airfield.

Incidentally, the factory manager Otto Kohl is being targeted but no decision has been taken, if, how and when he will be kidnapped, I have yet to get the information on their thinking.

Klaus Gunter, the scientist who was and still is, working on the fuel and its pump system, claims to be almost there. He is trying to find the perfect answer to enable a rocket to fly to any country in the world. He is in hiding, as his 'Know How' is wanted by so many countries and they will go to great lengths to find him and persuade him to work for them.

We all know the type of persuasion some countries would use.

This information is like a hot potato, I want to sell it all quickly. I will call back in two days."

With that the phone went dead.

Lance discussed the phone call with Ivan, trying to make a decision if it is important or not. "Lance, it is very serious but while it concerns the Russian sector, I can't see how the Allies can combat the Russians action.

The dismantling was not in the agreement at the Yalta conference but Russia is determined to keep Germany weak, hoping they can gradually take control of the whole of Berlin. The plan was agreed on was to denazification and demilitarize Germany and help the country to prosper with a growing economy to become a democratic country once more.

How much money is Rook asking for this information?"

"He is asking 600 U.S. Dollars."

"Right, Lance, Contact Colonel Clarke and discuss the phone call with him and make sure he is made aware of how serious it is and treat it as urgent but the information will cost them1200 U.S. Dollars." Lance telephoned Colonel Clarke and his reaction was one of pleasure to hear from Lance again, which pleased Lance. He explained the reason for his phone call without giving too much information away.

Colonel Clarke suggested they should meet up.

"If you can make it this evening, I will send a Jeep to pick you up I will need the address to pass on to the driver."

"Yes, I can make it tonight and he gave him his address. Shall we say six o'clock?"

"Good, I will leave instruction at the door of the club to enable you to enter without any problem."

The Jeep pulled up outside Lance's address at five thirty, the driver jumped down from the jeep and gave Lance an exaggerated salute. The journey took about thirty minutes, when he brought the jeep to a halt; Lance could hardly believe his eyes.

The front of the American Club and the foyer was as one would expect to see in one of the American cities. Beautifully painted and festooned with coloured electric light bulbs. Lance mounted the steps to the entrance. The man on the door asked Lance's name and he immediately escorted him into the club and announced his arrival. An American officer approached him.

"Are you Lance?"

"Yes, and you are?"

"I am Colonel Clarke but to you I am Max. Have you eaten yet?"

"No, the chef in our outfit is unreliable, his watch always has different time to everyone else, especially when it comes to breakfast." Said Lance laughing and Max joined in and it is obvious they will become permanent friends.

"Would you like a beer or we have a good selection of wines and a varied menu?"

Max guided Lance to a table in the corner of the room away the tables with people eating or drinking. The waiter brought two bottles of beer and Max signed the chit and he poured a glass each.

"Cheers, Lance",

"Good health Max" and they both took a drink from their glass.

"Now what are you being so secretive about Lance?"

"We had a telephone message from an international spy telling us that the Russians are going to dismantle a large engineering factory and transport all the machinery and machine tools to Russia and they intend to use slave labour by using the German engineers who worked in the factory.

The factory they intend to dismantle is the one that made the V2 Rockets, with which they bombarded England with at the latter part of the war. The Russians are anxious to discover how the rockets are constructed and the propulsion system.

Several countries want all the details but we have first choice, the cost is 1200 U.S. Dollars and we have two days to decide. The fuel and system man is in hiding because he has been threatened and he is wanted by several countries because of his 'Know How'. He foolishly boasted he could perfect a fuel and a system to enable a rocket to travel and be guided to reach any country in the world.

That Max is what I wanted to pass on to you but where, how and when, is what the money is for. I personally consider it to be very serious."

"You are so right Lance, I too regard it to be very serious but will the Brigadier forgo his game of bridge to even give it any consideration, I will run it past him, if, he dismisses it out of hand I will pass it on to a higher level. I have your phone number Lance; I will give you a call. Now we have met, do keep in touch."

They had finished their meal and a bottle of wine, Max got up from the table and went outside, he came back and told Lance that the driver is outside with his jeep. They shook hands and Lance climbed into the jeep and was waved off by Max.

The following morning the phone rang, the caller asked to speak to Lance.

"Lance speaking,"

"Morning Lance this is Max, just a quickie. There's quite a rumpus going on at the White House. It appears Senator Carter has learned of the circumstances leading up to the death of his son Robert and how the death threat aimed at Robert was ignored. Brigadier Brook has been taken to task and is being replaced. Pay Rook and I will forward the 1200 to your office but I want all the details for our money. Keep your powder dry Lance."

Max was laughing as he put the phone down.

*

Nathan Garland put the phone back on its cradle and heaved a great sigh, he had just received news he didn't want to hear. His job as Home Secretary of Great Britain is beginning to take a toll on his health.

He picked up his red scramble phone and dialed Number 10 Downing Street. A young lady answered the phone and after obtaining the necessary password, she passed him over to the Prime Minister.

"Hello Nat"

"How can I help?"

"I have received news that the Russians are going to dismantle the V2 Rocket engineering factory just outside Berlin and transport the machinery and the all the machine tools to Russia by air."

"Nat, this is all wrong, Russia is playing a dangerous game, during the conference in Yalta, it was agreed to remove the threat of further conflicts and help Germany to become a democratic country with a healthy economic growth planned for the future. From where or from whom did you get this information?"

"John, you should know that I am not at liberty to tell you, it would put my agent at risk. If an agent is identified, he or she becomes a target, this has happened before, when the name is released they do not survive. I will keep you informed as and when I receive any information."

Chapter 9

The Russians rounded up a team of 20 Germans to deal with the erection of lifting gear capable of lifting heavy machinery. The plan is that a crane is to be erected at the beginning of the runway at the local airfield to enable machinery to be put on board an aircraft and flown to Russia. The German team was taken to a factory on the outskirt of Berlin that had manufactured the V2 Rocket and was instructed to dismantle all the machinery and machine tools in the factory. The Germans were very much against this plan of stripping down and removing their lifeline for the future, the man put in charge of this operation had been the works manager. The senior Russian officer had insisted that Otto Brunner should be in charge, the manager lives in the American sector but his parents and his family all live in the Russian sector, pressure could be brought to bear making him do as he is told.

*

Lance contacted Rook asking to trace Otto's home address; I will pay you 50 American Dollars for this information.

"Sorry Lance, I will attempt to find the address you ask for but it will cost you 100 as it is possible that I will have to buy this information." Lance was glad he only suggested 50, otherwise Rook would have asked for 150.

Several days later, Rook phoned Lance telling him to go to a small café-bar two streets behind his building. "The owner is called Bruno, buy a cup of coffee and ask him if he has any message for Lance, he will nod but he will not give you an envelope containing the address until you pass him an envelope containing the 100Dollars." Lance smiled "Thanks Rook."

Lance walked round the back street until he found the small café, he walked through the door and looked round, what a sleazy dump, the floor hadn't been cleaned for weeks but all the shelves containing the crockery looked spotlessly clean. There several locals sat around watching his every move.

"Are you Bruno?"

"Yes, and you are?"

"Have you a message for Lance?"

Bruno poured out Lance's coffee, putting it on the counter.

"Yes, you have something for me?"

Lance handed the envelope and sat down to drink his coffee while Bruno went into the back to count the money and found it to be correct. He came back and handed Lance an envelope he had called for, it was Otto's home address.

The address was in the American sector; Lance set off to visit Otto. Otto was very surprised to find Lance on his doorstep and he made Lance very welcome when he pulled out a bottle of Malt whisky. Over a drink they discussed the possibility of something going wrong to prevent the machinery being flown to Russia.

The thing that bothered Otto was if he was found to be at fault for any happening, how that would affect his family's food supplies.

"Otto, give me their address and I will make sure they get supplies, I promise you that Otto."

Otto wrote his wife's address on a small piece of paper and handed it to Lance "I trust you with my children's future, don't let me down. I have never met you before but I somehow do trust you."

Ivan being a Russian Army Officer visited Otto's family in the Russian sector taking two food hampers and money to Otto's wife Greta. She wrote a letter addressed to Otto thanking him for the food, money and adding her expression of love and how he is missed.

On his return, he gave Lance the letter which he delivered the same evening. Lance smiled at Otto's misty eyed reaction as he read the letter, he read it several times and he then carefully folded it and put it in his pocket.

"Thanks Lance, it is great to hear from my family and the food will be a good help." Otto organized the steel girders and the many parts of machinery needed to assemble the lifting gear to ensure it will all operate in the correct manner, he also ordered two water bowsers each containing approximately 2000 litres. The Russian officer queried the bowsers until he was told they were for mixing the concrete but he was still skeptical on the amount of water required but Otto pointed out that he was in charge of the job. The bowsers were ordered and delivered.

The German team of engineers worked at a very slow pace, so much so, the Russian officer kept going into the factory, trying to push them to work faster. One of the larger steel turning beds was all disconnected and a flat low loader was driven into the works and the powerful overhead crane lifted it from the factory floor on to the wagon. The team was then taken to the airfield to start work on the lifting gear. Otto and his fellow engineers studied the situation but the majority was opposed to their equipment going to Russia and this caused a little friction among the team, although most of the team did not enjoy what they were doing but this was the only way their families would receive food. The German team was forced to work late into the night to excavate the soil and get the steel girders and the wooden rafters in place and then pour the concrete into the footings to set overnight. They were ordered to report early the following morning to start erecting the crane to be used the following day. The Russians thought it would be wise to give the concrete footings two days to dry out and settle.

As instructed they all arrived at the airfield very early and started removing the wooden spars and pieces of steel girders not used. A big wagon arrived with all the machine parts to assemble the crane but no weight or pressure was to be put on the footings and they all had their fingers crossed that all will go well the next day. When Otto and his team was sure that nothing else could be done that day, they were allowed to go home but before they left the site, Otto insisted that the water bowsers were dragged next to the crane, just incase either of them were stolen during the night as he is responsible for them.

The German team reported early in the second morning ready for when the plane lands and the low loader with the machinery from the factory was on site. They heard an aircraft approaching, when it came in sight they all wondered how on earth it was going to land on such a small airfield, it was obvious that the craft had been specially built to transport heavy loads, it was huge. The plane landed and the Russian officer instructed the wagon driver from the factory to bring the wagon closer to the crane. Two officers from the aircraft came to inspect the machinery and they put their flat topped trolley with ten rubber wheels alongside the crane, hoping it will be strong enough to withstand the weight while being dragged aboard the aircraft. The crane's engine was started up and the crane driver lowered the cables to be attached to the machinery. The steel cables were all placed in what they considered the correct balancing point. The crane driver then just raised the gantry to tauten the cables, when every one was satisfied with the balance of the cables, the crane driver was told to lift the machinery from the wagon and lower it on to the smaller trolley. The crane raised the machine, it was a few feet above the wagon when it started swinging, the bystanders quickly stepped back as the momentum appeared to increase and suddenly the crane toppled forward crashing on to the wagon and the trolley, Otto and his team started cheering. When the Russians inspected the crane, the base of the crane was still attached to the footing which should have anchored the crane had come away, the large hole was full of mud and water, the water from the bowsers had been piped to drain into the large hole during the night and the footings had come away still attached to a large complete block of steel and concrete. The Russian officer rushed over to Otto, his face went from red to purple, it is your fault and it is a deliberate act. The plane took off without its cargo, it was obvious heads will roll.

The Russian officer turned to Otto, pulled out his revolver and shot Otto dead. The group of Germans surrounded the Russian and he was killed, they removed the large inspection plate at the top of one of the bowsers and pushed the dead Russians body inside and then replaced the plate. The authorities would never understand what happened to the officer and it would be many months before they investigate a problem with the bowser that they will find his body and no one can then be held responsible.

The interpreter would offer no explanation, he was German.

Lance received a phone call from Rook; he related all that had happened at the airfield when the plane came to pick up the machinery. Rook chuckled as he told the story to Lance. "It is unfortunate that Otto was shot dead. He was quite a character and very well liked by his countrymen. I bet they will have a shock when they do find the body in the bowser."

When Rook put the phone down, Lance telephoned Max; he thought it laughable, although Lance was pleased with outcome, he was deeply sorry for Otto's family and he will keep his promise to Otto.

Chapter 10

Frank, Beth and their two children Maisie and Lewis were sat enjoying an evening meal when the phone started to ring, it made them jump. Frank went into the hall, lifted the receiver and a voice said

"Hello Frank."

"Hello Bob, I am so pleased to hear from you again."

"You won't be when I tell you why I am ringing you Frank"

"The old farm owner has died and his daughter assumed she would take over the farm but her brother has come out of the woodwork and is claiming the farm as his inheritance.

He is claiming that all the cottages and houses on the farmland must pay a ground rent; anyone who doesn't agree can remove their property or sell it to him at a nominal price. That would mean a knockdown price. He would like all the property owners to attend a meeting next week. Can you make it?"

"I certainly will my solicitor assured me that the price I paid for the cottage included the freehold of the land it stood on." Beth went to her parents to ask them if they would be kind enough move into their house to care for the children, to enable her and Frank to attend the meeting in France. They jumped at the chance to care for their grandchildren.

Beth was a little apprehensive about going, it appears that the farmer's son Charles has made this decision and he will not be persuaded not to insist on his planned income.

Two days later they left their home to journey to France and the trip was anything but enjoyable, they both suffered with the rough ferry crossing.

Arriving at Bob's cottage, Bob and Mary were delighted to see them and insisted that they should stay with them. Beth agreed as it will save going to the trouble of lighting the Aga for the central heating and airing their cottage. So, it was agreed and they decided to go into the village for their evening meal and meet some of the villagers who will be attending the meeting the following day.

Mary was so pleased and excited to have company and she regarded Beth as a good friend. The meeting was discussed at length and they were doubtful if they would be able to change the farmer's son's mind but the general feeling was, we must try.

*

They were all up bright and early the morning of the meeting and it was again discussed over breakfast table. Several of the villagers had come up with their own tactics hoping to make the meeting go their way but Bob and Frank were doubtful. After breakfast they got tidied up, left the cottage and joined the group of people walking towards the small barn, which, had been set up ready for the meeting. They were all surprised with the barns condition; it had been repaired and painted in such a way it amazed them as to how the farmer had managed to get the materials, which, other people were unable to obtain.

When they entered the barn, they found there were no chairs but a small platform had been erected at one end of the barn, obviously there for Charles to stand on. The people chattering echoed in the barn, suddenly it went quiet. Charles came swaggering into the barn and jumped up onto the platform.

"Thank you ladies and gentlemen for coming to this meeting, the reason for this meeting is to advise you of the changes that are to take place, my father allowed a lot of people take him for a fool.

I am going to put a stop to all you people building and living on my land free, yes it is my land now my father has passed on.

Linnet, my sister, thought she was going to inherit the farm but she is mistaken." Charles attitude towards the people attending the meeting was one of arrogance.

"The cottages around the farm and the four houses will have to pay a yearly ground rent; you cannot object or refuse to pay as this is the law. If however, any tenant refuses to pay, I will have them evicted and sell their property. This applies to a neighbouring farm, which I find is also on my land."

The meeting became chaotic, all shouting at the same time, one man jumped on to the platform trying to control the meeting asking them to speak one at a time.

The first person to step forward surprised everyone in the barn, it was Jacques. He walked up to the platform, pointed at Charles and shouted.

"He shot and killed my parents and then shot me as I ran away from him. This was one of his bullets," removing his cap; they could see his scarred head and face.

"Good Lord, he can speak."

The people in the barn started shouting and surging towards Charles.

He raised his arms, Stop, "I was made to shoot them by Françoise" and he never said anymore, a gunshot echoed in the barn and Charles was dead before he hit the floor, some person in the barn had shot Charles, to prevent him naming the man who had been an informer during the German occupation. The barn was in such an uproar it was difficult to ascertain from which area the gunshot came.

The police and an ambulance were quickly on the scene, the police instructed everyone to remain in the barn until their names and addresses have been taken by one of the police officers present. The body of Charles was covered with a sheet and placed on a gurney and wheeled away.

A tearful Linnet climbed on to the platform indicating with her hands to calm down the crowd in the barn and it all went quiet.

"I did not agree with Charles, there will be no ground rent to be paid, in fact, according to my father, the Freehold was included in the purchase price paid for the property. Please, go away and forget this meeting was ever called." She then stepped down, sat on the floor weeping.

Jacque was hysterical; "I did not shoot him, I haven't got a gun"

Frank went over to him and tried to console him but thinking that Jacque would have had every right to have done so but it was obvious that the boy was not responsible. Looking round Frank couldn't guess who would want Charles dead.

The police herded them all to one side of the barn to have all their details listed in a notebook. The people who had travelled to attend the meeting were told not to leave the area. Beth telephoned her mother asking her to stay with the children, her mother readily agreed when Beth explained the circumstances.

The police spent the next few days interviewing and questioning the people who were in the barn at the time of the shooting.

They gradually untangled secrets of a black-market ring during the occupation and Charles was one of the leading members but the man in charge was Francoise Gerard, who is now the local Mayor.

All the collaboration he did with the occupying forces came to light and Jacques father was about to expose him when Charles shot him on the Mayor's instruction.

When Francoise's house was searched they found a German luger hand gun and ammunition. Under intensive interrogation he admitted the killing. The villagers were pleased when the police got to the bottom of the shooting; everyone was looking over their shoulder wondering who could be responsible and who was next.

Bob and Mary made Frank and Beth very comfortable but they were pleased when the police allowed all the visitors to return home. Beth was not looking forward to the return trip on the ferry; her tummy was still queasy after the sea sickness bout she had on the trip a couple of weeks ago.

Chapter 11

Lance smiled as he replaced the phone back on its cradle; his smile disguised his puzzled expression. Rook had phoned Lance, hoping to lay claim to a future payment for information when he is able to provide the complete picture.

"Lance, the fact that you have installed Klaus in what you consider to be a safe house in the American sector is a big joke. It is common knowledge who he is, where he is living and why he is in hiding."

"I heard a whisper that he and his house are under constant surveillance, noting his every movement and a full report is to be sent, to where? The people who are watching him are reported to belong to a large organization controlled by a man named either Wong or Wang. He is a very powerful arms dealer and he is trying to expand into the drug import and export business. He is to be handled with great care; he has so many Government Ministers on his payroll and has become untouchable although his organization is linked to many murders."

"It is his people who are planning to kidnap Klaus, how and when have not been decided yet. When they do decide, I'll be told but it will cost me a lot of money, as I'll have to buy this information."

"Wong firmly believes he can blackmail the whole world knowing he can attack any country in the world using Klaus's Rockets, fuel and guidance system."

"What is his nationality Rook?"

"I saw him once; he keeps out of the limelight. He has an oriental look about him, perhaps Chinese but as you know they are all facially similar from that part of the world."

Lance decided to telephone a friend of his in London to check on Wang or Wong, an arms dealer who operates out of China or Vietnam

His friend rang back an hour later.

"Lancelot, you have a big problem if you are crossing swords with the Thai Wong gang. Wong operates from three different islands. Every time the authorities send in a force to invade one of the islands hoping to capture Wong, the gang just disappears like steam in the atmosphere, very elusive. It is obvious some one on his payroll tips him off." Lance discussed his information with Ivan, he was at a loss which way to advise Lance to go, Klaus is at risk of being kidnapped and taken to the kidnappers country or are they preparing to sell him to the highest bidder but who are they? Lance telephoned Max and gave him the full details, here again Max was not sure what steps to take but he fully intended to look into the question of the American safe houses, which, according to the most recent report, the safe houses are no longer safe, every one knows about Klaus and he is being regarded as a valuable target. "Lance shall we move Klaus to another house or put two lookalikes in the house or should we put lookalikes in several of our so called safe houses just to cause confusion?" The CIA supplied several people who had been trained in Klaus's looks and mannerisms, such as when he removes his glasses he tilts his head to the right and twirls his glasses holding the right hand spectacle arm. As he stands up his always rubs his right hip. The American authorities were getting very concerned by the number of people watching two of their houses and decided to increase their protection team to be on 24 hour surveillance. Lance was convinced who ever kidnapped Klaus wouldn't need any form of persuasion to get him to help; he would only be too pleased to continue his work, which is his life.

In spite of the additional cover, two small slim men dressed completely in what looked like black hooded siren suits which, covered their heads and face with slit for their eyes, entered one of the houses and kidnapped Klaus; at least they thought it to be Klaus. It was when they took their prisoner into the laboratory it was obvious that the man was completely lost and the scientist in charge immediately realized the mistake. Sadly, the man's body was later discovered by the CIA with an executioners shot at the back of the head.

The other CIA people acting as the lookalikes became very nervous; they hadn't realized they were putting their lives at risk when helping to foil a kidnapping plot. They thought the object was just to cause confusion and this lapse in the security has caused them to break ranks and decided not to take any part unless the threat to their lives was removed. Klaus called his scientist team together and told them how they all appear to be under a threat. "I don't really know who is trying to kidnap us, there are many rumours running around about various gangs are trying to capture us and sell us, or should I say, they want our knowledge of how we have perfected the guided system and how the fuel replaces itself as it is used. I have been approached by the American authorities asking if we and our families would like to be taken to the United States to carry on with our work. I would like you to discuss this proposition with your families and it is most important that it is treated with the upmost secrecy for our own safety. I have to give an answer in two days, so gentlemen; you have two days to decide."

Several days later Klaus called his team together again to get their decision on the American offer, they all said they would like to accept the opportunity to go to America. The only query was from Fritz who was concerned for his two boys regarding their education. "Fritz, you have no fear, all of our children will be placed in the best school or college the choice will be yours. Naturally, they will have to attend an intensive language course, which will be laid on for them. I have been assured, whatever reasonable requests you make, they will be met." Six o'clock in the morning, Lance was in bed fast asleep when he was awakened by his telephone ringing, he picked up the phone he immediately recognized Max's voice. "Lance, the Russians have stopped the train bringing supplies for our occupation forces. They attached a train and shunted it back beyond their border to the Eastern Sector of Berlin. We now don't have access to our section. These supplies were not only for our forces but also for the population in the Western section of Berlin, incidentally, they have closed the road access and all of the waterways, which, only leaves the three, twenty mile wide air corridors. A meeting is being arranged to discuss this problem, whether or not we can carry enough supplies by air is another story. Joe Stalin is trying to starve the allies out of Berlin and he then hopes to take over the city as a whole." An emergency meeting was called and all the Allies high ranking officers were present, to discuss what measures to take to combat the latest Russian move. A senior senator who was an adviser to the President of America was flown into Germany to chair the meeting. "Gentlemen, Russia has closed all our access to Berlin, they closed the roads and waterways, which, is in direct contrary to the Yalta agreement. We are faced with a big problem, not only do we have to feed our occupying forces but approximately two million population of Berlin. The Russians are playing a dangerous game by trying to starve the Allies out of Berlin; the Berliners will be terrified with the prospect of the Russian army taking charge in view of their history of cruelty and rape. I can tell you President Roosevelt, says, we will not desert Berlin, so gentlemen, we have to come up with foolproof plan.

The situation we are faced with is this, the only access into Berlin is by air, we have three 20mile wide air corridors no doubt if we use them the pilots of the aircraft will get some unpleasant activity from the Soviet air force. It will be a mammoth task flying in amount of supplies required into our western sector. We have the use of two airfields, Templelhof and Gatow but neither were built to accept such a high volume of traffic, it will be mammoth task to handle such a large volume and transport the goods to a distribution centre. I am in no position to say what aircraft are available and the amount of goods each aircraft can carry. Apart from transporting food, we will have to bring in tons of coal necessary to keep the Berliners warm and to supply industry to enable them to carry on working. Unfortunately, the electricity plants are in the Soviet sector and we have already experienced problems of spasmodic supplies outside of our control. Before I came to this meeting, I visited a distribution centre and they are concerned how their stocks are reducing at an alarming rate. In view of this, we may have to introduce rationing."

A senior German officer present said, "The Berliners would happily accept rationing, rather than be controlled by the Russians."

"Right gentlemen, go away now and we will meet up again tomorrow morning at 10 am, in the meantime consider our options very carefully. I must confess that I feel a little desperate at the moment but I sure we will come up with a satisfactory answer. Gentlemen, we must find a way to overcome our problem."

*

The following morning the meeting was reconvened as planned, the American Chairman stood up. "Gentlemen, I have listened to all of your ideas and comments and the common consensus is that the Airlift is the only option open to us, this will amuse the Russians as they are confident that we can't hope to fly in enough supplies. In fact, they are preparing to move in as we leave but this isn't going to happen. I will personally interview the staff and delegate the person who will be responsible for each stage of the operation."

One of the Air chiefs stood up to say. "I am very concerned with high buildings around the airfields which will make the low approach to touch down necessary; due to a heavily laden large aircraft it will be rather difficult and dangerous."

"The pilots will have to cope with all the difficult situations" said the chairman.

Chapter 12

The first aircraft to land carrying supplies was American, one of the senators present panicked; he started shouting that the unloading was taking far too long. He was insistent that they must have a turn round of maximum fifteen minutes otherwise the aircraft will be stacked up in the air waiting to land and apart from this, the turn round must be sharp to transport sufficient supplies. The senior German office present suggested, using German labour and pay them by increasing their ration of food. The American officer agreed, "Thanks, that is a good idea."

"Not at all, they realize the food is for them as well as your forces."

The aircraft were refueled and was to wait on a small runway adjacent to the main runway so as not to cause any hold up. The pilot of one of these aircraft Ben Langer was told he would be taking passengers with him back to the U.S.A.

Klaus's team and their families were gathered together; fortunately they had previously been advised to be ready to move at one hours notice. They were brought out to the aircraft and as they boarded the aircraft they were all greeted by Ben while their luggage was put in the hold. Several asked how long the flight would take but he was unable to give an answer, it all depends on when he will be allowed to take off and he knew that they will be landing in Scotland to refuel and a meal had been arranged for them.

Klaus's team was all excited about going to America, the only thing they knew about America is what they had seen on films and many of them had never flown before. Klaus's family flatly refused to join him.

When they landed in Scotland they were escorted off the plane and taken into the VIP lounge near the departure area. They were amazed and delighted with the food and amount that was offered to them. After one hour they and twenty five additional passengers were asked to make their way back to the aircraft and they boarded and got settled for a long haul. The plane set off bound for the USA, looking out of the windows they could see the mainland disappearing and in its place came the Atlantic Ocean. Suddenly Ben the pilot, became alarmed, the engines were losing power and he had difficulty in maintaining height, he immediately contacted the ground control advising of his situation and his position. The engines stopped, he wrestled with the controls trying to glide but he was unsuccessful and they were dropping like a stone. The plane hit the sea at a very high speed and the aircraft just disintegrated, passengers and bits of the aircraft were catapulted over a large area. Sadly, no one could expect to survive such an impact. The ground controllers alerted ships in that area but they did not receive any reports of floating wreckage or bodies.

"Lance received a phone call from Max telling him of the disaster and no bodies or wreckage had been spotted or found. Washington is in an uproar and whole system of the US security is in question. An in depth investigation is be carried out, particularly into the recorded messages received from the pilot Ben Langler who was an experienced pilot.

There was an instrument on board being experimented by Klaus that was capable of closing down aircraft engines and this must have had been activated from the ground or a ship in that vicinity. This instrument had been a brain child of Klaus and it had never been tested outside the laboratory and it had been a very closely guarded secret. The aircraft was in the worst possible position for this tragedy to happen, mid Atlantic. Don't be surprised if the CIA contacts either Ivan or yourself asking for your help to trace from where the secret information is being obtained and passed on to whom? It might be worth paying Rook to nose around, just a thought Lance. Perhaps it would be better to wait until they contact you and then you can spend their money that is if you are prepared to undertake such a task. They might also ask you to look into the loss of supplies that arrive at the airport and then disappear on route to the distribution centre; so far they have been unable to trace the leakage. All the vans used are the same vehicle model and painted a bright yellow and the drivers all wear the same uniform."

"Right Max, I will contact you if they should phone us, In fact, the black market has had an increase in its selection lately."

Thai Wang called his senior henchmen together to discuss their next money making project. He told them that there was too much street trade of drugs and the streets are being flooded with cigarettes by the US service men in Berlin. "I have bought a large house which, was damaged during an allied air attack. The entrance is to be left to look like a derelict building site. Inside, I want a small area luxuriously laid out with a well stocked bar, three massage parlours and three or four bedrooms and we will open it up as a Brothel." One of the team asked, "How could we attract suitable younger women to take part, if so, at what cost?"

Thai smiled. "After spending two weeks dealing with the inside of the building, I have explained how I want the interior. I need you to locate suitable young ladies or perhaps widows with a young family. Nurture her friendship and supply her with a small amount of goods and also add a couple of candy sticks or chocolate for the small children. Once she has got used to a decent table, gradually reduce the amount of supplies you give her."

"If however, she should ask for more, you can tell her, or should I say, persuade her to work for me in the building and she will be paid with ample food supplies. Most families are really hungry and this should provide you with a lever to get her to agree. Interference from any person or from the gangs which are roaming the streets, contact me immediately and they will be dealt with. After a while no one, even senior Service Officers will give you any trouble if you are wearing your green lapel badge, which, will be supplied."

Two weeks later Thai visited the site and he was far from happy with the progress, the conversion was taking far too long to his way of thinking, he was not satisfied and called for more men to be employed to quicken the pace. The increase in workmen made a dramatic effect on the work schedule, Thai was notified that the building was ready for his inspection, which he carried out but for a very few minor adjustments he was quite happy. He had been a little concerned whether or not the delivery of goods might create some speculation but as it was in such a broken down area no one attached any importance to the coming and goings of the delivery lorries.

Chapter 13

Heine targeted a very attractive young lady to carry out the plan Thai had instructed. He visited a small café bar where a dance was taking place, he ordered himself a drink and he saw this young lady standing by herself, he went to her and asked to dance with him. He learned that she worked at the café as a cleaner and sometimes as a member of the bar staff. From then they spent the evening dancing together in fact; they talked and became quite friendly. Her name was Bella but avoided telling her surname which didn't bother Heine, there is such a mix of nationals in Berlin at the present time. From that night on they spent time together dancing or visiting amateur plays or band shows. After about ten days Bella invited Heine to meet her family, which, consisted of, her mother, mother in law and two children. Unfortunately, the men folk had been killed during the war. Bella's family were astounded when Heine arrived armed with a box of goods and candy for the children, it was so obvious they were living on the bread line, the elderly ladies going without to feed the youngsters. He was welcomed with open arms as food like this, they had not seen for a year or so and he realized Thai's plan had every chance of succeeding. On his next visit he took a lot less and the ladies were disappointed but it was to plan. The next visit he took nothing which again was a disappointment and this happened on his next two visits. Bella nervously approached Heine as to why the supplies had dried up. He told her that he had been unable to obtain any supplies but she would get ample if she worked in Thai's House as it had been named.

He took her along to meet the lady in charge named Lottie. She took Bella into an adjoining room to conduct an interview, Heine was waiting outside, when red faced Bella came charging out of the room and went outside. Lottie followed Bella out of the room, she looked at Heine. "She will come round to our way of thinking when her family is hungry."

Heine went outside to find Bella, when he found her. "What on earth is a matter Bella?"

"Do you know what sort of job she offered me?"

"I have no idea Bella."

"She wanted me to work there entertaining gentlemen I was to have sex with them or anything else the client wanted me to do. In return, I would be paid with food supplies, candy and chocolate for my children."

"Sorry Bella, I didn't know what the job entailed and she told you that you would be paid with food supplies, wine, and chocolate for the children. Not a bad wage." Heine burst out laughing and Bella joined in. "I was married and I have two children, so I know what it is all about."

On returning home she discussed her visit with her two mothers, they too started laughing. Her mother in law said. "If I was younger and lusted after and I too could get supplies, I would be very interested." They started laughing again and thought it hilarious.

Heine called later that day he apologized, claiming he didn't know what jobs were on offer. He went empty handed, much to the disgust of the children but he explained that supplies are very short at the moment. Bella's mother -in- law told him their rations had been reduced due to the bad weather which is affecting flying conditions. He just smiled. Encouraged by her two mothers, Bella went back to Thai's House to speak to Lottie the lady in charge. When she arrived she was invited to join another young lady and Lottie proceeded to show them all round the building. They started with the Massage Parlour and then into the Bar area, the bedrooms certainly surprised them, the bedrooms were really exceptional, the colours and the décor generally, was out of this world. They were both very impressed with whole setup.

"Ladies, I want you to go away and think about our offer and I would like an answer in two days, as I have to arrange for you both to attend a clinic to be examined by a lady doctor to make sure you are both in a healthy condition, before you start work."Bella and Greta left the house and went to a coffee bar to talk over what they had been told. They both knew that if their families were to survive the food shortages, this was the only job available to them. "Right let us go back and say yes to her offer." They returned to the House to accept the offer of a job and Lottie said. "I must lay it on the line. Some of your clients might be a little nervous it could be their first encounter with the opposite sex; you will have to take the initiative and lead them into their new world. With such clients you can save a lot of time if you learn your trade correctly. You will find some of your clients will need varied sort of sexual activity, it might be normal sex or perhaps oral sex maybe some kinky sex act known to them Goodluck. Your payment of food supplies is a better proposition than taking money, the amount of money you would receive would only pay for a fraction of the food in the box."

*

Bella made a point of contacting Greta as she was more experienced of the two as she had worked in such an environment before. They had both agreed to go ahead and work in Thai's House and Greta promised Bella that she would help her if she came up against any problems, such as awkward clients or offensive ones but they had been assured, security staff would be on hand. When they went to the house, they were taken by car to the clinic where the lady doctor was waiting for them. She examined them individually and took blood to have analyzed. They were taken to a room and given the option of tea, coffee or an alcoholic drink, whichever they preferred. Forty five minutes later the doctor came into the room and told them that were both acceptable but if they decided to go ahead working as an entertainer to the gentlemen, they would have to return to this clinic every month or so to ensure they are clean and healthy. They returned to Thai's house and gave the lady in charge their clean bill of health from the doctor. It was arranged they would start work in two days time. Bella made a point of contacting Greta to ensure they started work together, Greta was the more experienced of the two.

Bella was very nervous and apprehensive about starting work today but she had planned to meet up with Greta, Greta is a tall, slim, blue eyes and blonde hair a perfect specimen of a true Aryan. While they were waiting to be allocated their room Greta told Bella that she had been recruited and placed in the Nazi baby farm, whilst there she had two babies. She had no idea who the fathers were or where the babies are now, they were taken away at birth, I have tried to trace them but all the doors have been closed and I had to admit defeat. They were taken to the bedrooms allocated to them, Greta and Bella's rooms were adjacent with a connecting door.

*

The first client Bella received was the very same boy that Lotto had described. A tall slim dark haired young man, he was more nervous than Bella and as described by Lottie he could be dealt with very quickly. He nervously looked around and then at Bella and smiled.

"Hello, and who are you?"

"My name is Gary." Right, just sit down Gary. He sat down still looking uncomfortable.

Bella stood behind him and gently stroked his neck, bending down she lifted his shirt, gradually lifting it over his head. Bella got him in a standing position to remove his shirt, she gently moved him to sit on the bed. Bella laid him down on

to the bed and kissed his arms and chest. She removed his shoes and socks and then released his trouser belt and very gently started sliding his trousers down kissing his body as she lowered the waistband down. He raised his body to allow Bella to slide the trousers right down and remove them. He lay on the bed just wearing his underpants and it was a movement in that garment, she could tell that her gentle approach was having the desired effect. She removed the last remaining garment, kissing and fondling him, as she did so Gary just laid on the bed moaning. Bella took off her flimsy robe and lay on the bed with him. As she went to move on him, his moaning increased and his face was wreathed with a large smile right across his face. Bella knew she was too late to help him and smiled to herself. Bella got off the bed and gently sponged Gary before helping him dress.

Gary left the room smiling and whistling. Bella thought, I hope all my clients are that easily pleased.

The next gentleman directed to Bella's room was Man Mountain. The man was at least six feet six inches tall and heavily built, bald headed and sported a large bushy beard. When Bella opened her door she was astounded at the man's physique, he had to bend to enter the room. Greta was just seeing her client off when she saw this very large man enter Bella's room, she started laughing to herself. When Bella greeted the man and politely asked his name, he just mumbled "Simon."

She sat him down and then made him a cup of coffee, as she handed the cup and saucer to him, as he took the cup from her he was trembling so badly, he spilled the coffee in the saucer with the cup rattling. Bella felt sorry for the man, he was trembling with little control. While he was drinking his coffee Bella removed his shoes and socks, then his tie and started to undress him. Bella was having a little trouble getting him to lie on the bed, Greta walked through the connecting door.

"Hello young man, if you are looking for excitement, you have come to the right place" Simon smiled for the first time and he appeared to relax, which, made it easier for Bella to continue undressing him, kissing and fondling at the same time. Greta helped doing the same thing. Bella and Greta stood either side of the bed and started easing the waistband of his underpants down very slowly, kissing and stroking the inside of his thighs and he responded. When they had finally removed his undergarment they looked at each other trying to keep a straight face but with laughter in their eyes. They had expected to see the size of his body reflected in the size of his manhood but it wasn't the case. They continued stroking and kissing and suddenly they saw a small area of skin move. They pounced on it but they hardly got going when he ejaculated and sat bolt upright.

Greta did the honours of cleaning him up with a sponge. He got off the bed laughing and singing and proceeded to dress himself. He was so pleased with himself. "Thank you ladies, you treated me like a man with needs, when I am forced to attend the hospital the nurses poke fun at me and call me a freak." he pulled out some money from his pocket and handed it to them, without further adue he walked out of the room and left by the side door of the building.

Lottie heard sheiks of laughter coming from Bella's room.

She rushed to the room.

"What on earth is going on?" Greta was wiping laughter tears from her eyes.

"Have you ever tried pushing a jelly baby into a Yale lock?"

"Good lord no." Greta looked up "We have." Lottie joined in the laughter, knowing full well to what they are referring. When Bella arrived home she was pleasantly surprised with the box of food that had been delivered that afternoon. It had instructions printed on the side of the box that the box is to be retained until the next delivery. In large writing it said, "This box must not be disposed of."

Chapter 14

Max telephoned Lance asking if he and Ivan were available if he and his associates could call later that day, Lance replied saying he would be pleased to meet them.

Three o'clock in the afternoon the office door bell rang, when Lance opened the door, he was surprised to see Max and he had four other people with him, three in uniform and one in civilian clothes. Lance took them into the main office and they were all very surprised and impressed how the office was fitted out with all the latest communication equipment. Lance got them all seated and proceeded to serve the drinks, he made a point of telling them that this whole operation is Ivan's brain child and Ivan is not able to understand all that is said in English but I will translate each way, just to make everyone comfortable.

Max introduced his fellow officers, the man in charge was the Head of the Allies intelligence team in Berlin and the other three in uniform were agents.

The senior man started the meeting, looking around he said, "Too many secrets from our meetings are being passed on to someone, by whom we don't know but it is essential we trace the source of the leakage."

"The instrument which destroyed Klaus's plane killing all its occupants was a very closely guarded secret, as far as we can gather, only eight people knew of its existence and apart from Klaus, two of these attended the trial in the laboratory.

When Klaus selected these two men, it was the two he trusted the most and they died with him in the crash. No way would they have given away secrets to kill themselves. The ray gun was used to activate the instrument on board, they must have known the correct co-ordinates of the planes direction and must have been a predetermined plan to place the untried gun under the exact flight path."

*

Looking at Lance, "Max has told us that you have contact with agents who can be bought to sniff out guarded secrets; I am giving Max free hand to make funds available to pay, whatever his name is. Ask him to visit the bars or however he operates. The other important problem is how supplies that are landed don't always arrive at the distribution centre. Every care has been taken, all the transport vehicles are the same and painted yellow and the drivers have been vetted and wear the same type of uniform but all this you know. One thing that is puzzling us is this, there is a lesser amount of our supplies being offered on the street black market but the same amount is still going astray. Every attempt must be made to stop this leakage." They all stood up, shook hands and Max and his team left.

*

Lance left messages around asking Rook to phone, he was not answering his phone in spite of Lance calling his number many times. Several days later Lance got a call from Rook. "Where on earth have you been, I have been trying to contact you?"

"I've been in hiding, I was blamed for the death of a Russian agent but they have now captured the culprit, so now I'm off the hook."

Lance outlined the lapse in the Allies security.

"You mean the rocket scientist who died in the air crash whilst on his way to USA?"

"Yes Rook, that is one of the problems, I want you to ask around and the other thing is how food supplies disappear between unloading the arriving aircraft into the van and a lesser amount arriving at the distribution centre."

"Lance, you are aware that I will have to buy this type of information and it doesn't come cheap."

"Rook, I am quite prepared to pay, just get me the information I need."

*

Rook contacted two of his friends and explained about the missing supplies and the question of secrets being leaked from the Allied meetings. Klaus's disaster was one secret that they thought had been closely guarded. It was arranged after spinning a coin, who would take on which task, providing they would be well paid. Rook told them the cash is on the table, if you can find the answers, payment will be good.

Rook said, "The one of you dealing with the supplies will be known as Jack and the other trying to find the secret leakage will be known as Bill, okay?" This amused Rook, he thought it would also appeal to Lance's sense of humour when he told him.

Lance smiled, "They are known as Jack and Bill, it is okay with me but keep in touch."

Jack started visiting Bars asking questions and finding that the goods on the black market were now very thin on the ground, in consequence, the shortage is reflected in the price, which, has risen dramatically. He managed to trace a friend of his whom he thought might help and throw some light on the situation. However, all he could tell Jack that some big man had taken over the stealing of supplies.

That evening Jack went to garage where two of the vans are garaged, he managed to open the garage door and went inside. Looking round he found the two vans parked in a corner, he stood and studied the vans and he could see no problem. The tailgate of one of the vans was unlocked so he opened it and crept inside the van. He froze as he heard footsteps coming his way, as the footsteps faded, he breathed out a deep sigh of relief. He took a torch out of his pocket and looked around inside the van. There were still a few empty cardboard boxes lying around, he avoided them to prevent making a noise. Looking around his eyes was drawn to the space above the driver's cabin. It had been closed off and two small doors cleverly fitted that at first sight they wouldn't register.

He climbed up to inspect, it was just as he expected , the doors opened to a expose a large area where supplies could be stored or should I say hidden until the vans arrive back at the garage. He photographed it and slowly opened the tailgate to get out of the van. As he was leaving the security man shouted, is somebody there and came dashing across to where Jack was hiding. The man looked around and after a while he returned to his small cabin. He reported his suspicions of an intruder to his boss the following morning but on checking they found nothing had been stolen.

Jack had the film developed and then contacted Rook, he showed the area where the stolen supplies are hidden until the van arrives back at the garage. "I will check on the vans when the next plane load of supplies arrives, I will go in the evening to check out the vans and anything else I can find." Rook contacted Lance telling him the full story, Lance was a little hesitant about passing the information on to Max, he did not feel comfortable with people he brought to his office a couple of weeks ago but he thought he should put Max completely in the picture as he was supplying the money.

*

The day the freight planes arrived, Jack watched the two vans leave the garage. Five hours later the vans returned to the garage and Jack planned to check on the van as he had told Rook he would but he wasn't aware that Rook had passed his intention down the line. When darkness fell, Jack dressed in suitable dark clothing, hoping he would be unnoticed. He found he garage door unlocked, he quietly opened the door and closed it behind him. He crept to one of the vans and he found the door locked, he moved to the next van and was able to open the tailgate he eased himself up into the van, checked the space above the driver's cabin but if it had been used there was no boxes in there now. As he jumped down out of the van, two men grappled him to the floor and tied his hands and feet.

"Did you find what you was looking for?"

He was bundled into a car and driven off.

Lance rang Rook, "Did Jack find any supplies in the small cupboard above the driver's cabin?"

"I don't know, he has not contacted me yet, in fact, I am getting concerned for his safety."

Max phoned Lance telling him a man's body had been found executed with a shot to the back of his head and his description appears to match Rooks agent, Jack.

"Max, if this is the case, to whom did you pass the information I gave you regarding his return visit last night?"

"The same people I brought to visit you."

"In that case, one of them is on the crooks payroll."

"That is most unlikely but it does point that way."

"Who was the man in charge of the group you brought along?"

"Brigadier Bolton."

"Is it possible to meet him again?"

"Yes I will arrange it for tomorrow afternoon."

As planned they all went to Brigadier's office. The Brigadier stood up.

"This meeting has been convened at the request of Lance; I am not too sure that his rank gives him the right to demand such a meeting." Lance stood up.

"The information obtained by an agent was very informative but to ensure he was on the right track, he decided to return two nights ago after the van had been used to unload an incoming flight. Gentlemen, each one here knew of his planned visit and one of you in this room passed this information on. This resulted in the agent being executed?"

The Brigadier shouted, "How dare you accuse one of my staff of passing on information."

"Brigadier, I have every right to accuse one of your staff present because one of them is a double agent and getting well paid."

"What right and what experience have you to act in this manner?"

"I was trained and I became a senior officer in the British Secret Service before being seconded into the RAF. If you doubt my ability, phone Colonel Snaith, he has an office in New Scotland Yard. What is more, one of your staff was seen drinking in a small sleazy bar with two of Thai Wong's gang. If the man has any decency, he will explain to rest of us why he was sharing the company of the enemy."

No one offered to admit to their indiscretion. As they were leaving the meeting, one leaned and whispered to Lance. "You sealed your fate."

Lance and Ivan sat discussing the happenings of the past few days; they both agreed that the supplies and secrets problems are entwined.

As they sat talking the phone rang, Ivan answered he turned round and handed the phone to Lance.

This is Rook, "Lance you must watch your back, it appears you have upset someone, it could be Thai Wong or one of his followers. Don't use your own car for a while, that is the method of assassination that has been used lately."

"Thanks Rook, I owe you one."

Lance telephoned Max. "Max before we talk, I insist what I going to tell you, remains between us at the moment.

Rook telephoned me and told me I have upset someone and must watch my back. The method of assassination Thai's gang has used recently is a bomb installed under the bonnet of the car and he advised me not to drive.

My plan is, I intend to use my car and park it in a suitable area for my enemies to deal with it, my technical team will check and if a bomb has been planted, defuse it and I will drive my car home. I gamble they will go into my garage and try to understand why the bomb didn't explode when I turned the ignition key. I will arrange for a reception committee to be in the garage to arrest them. We should then be able to find out who is behind the attempt on my life."

"It sounds a good plan Lance but you must take no chances. I have three people who can be made available to you and they are trustworthy, in fact I would trust them with my life and I did on one occasion." Lance telephoned three British Secret Service agents asking them to come to his office the following day and they were waiting on his doorstep for Lance to arrive, they sat and chatted and drank coffee, when they had finished drinking Lance looked up. "This is the reason for my calling you and he went through his plan with them and he gave each one a card with the index number of the car he will be driving. He told them the exact position where he would park his car the following day and he wants it kept under surveillance at all times, in fact, perhaps it would be better if you worked in shifts to avoid you getting bored and looking away, which, could cost me my life.

*

The following morning he went to an open car park and positioned his car as arranged, locked it and walked away. One of the agents sat watching but he could see no problem but suddenly he sat up with a jerk. Four men walked into the car park and started to wash a car two cars away from Lance's car. Having finished that car they moved on to Lance's car, they washed and leathered it then lifted the bonnet, this surprised the agent, how could he lift the bonnet lid with the car all locked up? All four were washing the underside of the bonnet lid the agent couldn't make out what they were up to because two leaned over the wings, to obscure any passer by seeing what they were doing. They opened the boot and went on washing and leathering. One of the men was leaning in the engine compartment pretending to wash but he was doing something else. The four men got into a car and drove off. When they were clear of the park the agent contacted the technician who was waiting around the corner and when he checked, he found a limpet type of bomb stuck on the bulkhead in the engine compartment in front of the driver. The bomb was defused; Lance drove his car back home straight into the garage and locked the garage doors leaving an agent inside the garage as arranged and one agent hidden outside at the rear of the garage.

As darkness was beginning to fall, the third agent joined his pal to hide at the rear of the garage. After two hours the agents and Lance began to think the gamble had not paid off but suddenly they heard footsteps on the gravel driveway and then they heard the garage doors being unlocked, how, have they unlocked the doors? Lance just shrugged his shoulders. Two men crept into the garage, again they were small and very slim wearing black hooded siren suits and one was carrying a toolbox. Then went up to the car and lifted the bonnet lid, they were busy for a few minutes, put the lid back down and prepared to leave, at this point the agent jumped from out of the darkness on one of them the other made a dash for it but he was wrestled to the ground by the two agents outside.

Lance contacted the RAF Police who came and arrested the two men and were taken to a security centre. When asked for whom they are working, they refused to answer. The sergeant in charge said, "Leave them here, they will tell us when they get hungry and thirsty." Lance didn't altogether agree with the suggested treatment but they would have killed him without any feeling at all in fact, they would probably look for a bonus from the person who ordered his death.

The following day, the sergeant rang Lance telling him the prisoners were ready to talk, what they are saying makes no sense to me.

Lance and Ivan went to the detention block, the sergeant greeted them. They were taken to a small cell like room with two chairs one side of a table and a single chair the other side. One of the suspects was brought into the room and was seated on the single chair.

Lance sat down and faced him. "Now, are you going to tell me what you were doing to my car and who are you working for?"

"My boss, Thai Wong instructed us to remove the limpet bomb attached to the bulkhead in front of the driver. It is not he who is trying to kill you; it is another group of people. If you wish to speak to Thai I have his phone number?" Lance was taken aback, if it isn't Thai Wong, who is it?

Lance decided to take the bull by the horns and phoned Thai and Thai invited him to meet him in his office. Lance jumped into his jeep, on loan from Max and went to meet Thai.

He entered the building and he was met by a young lady.

"Are you Lance?"

"Yes, Thai is expecting me."

"Follow me please." They walked along a long narrow passageway and she unlocked a door and entered a luxuriously furnished office, everything about the place smelled of money. A man rose from his chair behind a large desk, he was rotund figure with a round face. His hair was jet black and had been cut leaving the hair half an inch in length all over his scalp, in fact, his hair looked similar to hedgehogs spikes.

"Please sit down Lance; I am not stealing secrets or any of the supplies being flown into Berlin. I buy them on the Black Market to pay the girls operating Thai House as a Brothel. There I have told you of my activities, Drugs are no longer my thing or cigarettes. The real reason I wanted to speak to you, was to assure you that it is not my group trying to kill you. I have taken steps to prevent this happening. When your people defused the bomb to enable you to drive home, they did not see another man go back and reactivate it. My man went back again and removed all the wires. It was a case of follow my leader; imagine the number of people dealing with your car. Lance, look closer to your home to find your enemies. I am so pleased to have met you, I know a lot of people regard me as a crook but I just trying to earn a good living and accumulate enough money to enjoy a comfortable retirement." Thai rose from his chair putting out his hand to shake with Lance.

"Lance, remember what I said, look closer to your home to find your enemies." He left Thai's office feeling nonplussed, he thought, where do I go from here?

Lance discussed his meeting with Thai with Ivan, "What do we do now?"

"To be honest Lance I don't know. Who on earth would one our own want to sabotage our operation of helping the Berliners to stay alive."

Lance checked his phone and he found that Rook had left a message asking Lance to phone. Lance dialed the number and he heard Rook pick up the phone.

"Hello, Rook speaking."

"Hello Rook just returning your call."

"May I come to office, what I have to tell you, is too sensitive to discuss over the phone."

"Certainly Rook come round, I will put the coffee pot on."

"The door bell rang, Lance opened the door, and Rook offered his hand to shake with Lance." Lance was very surprised with Rook's appearance, he had a picture in his mind of Rook being a short heavily built figure but he was just the opposite. Rook stood six feet tall, athletic figure and a shock of black curly hair.

"Now Rook what is so important?"

"What I am going to tell you will cost 150 American Dollars, that is what the information cost me."

"I have the money Rook."

"I have been calling in a lot of favours from my friends and they have come up with a name of a man acting as a double agent and he is on Brigadier Bolton's staff. The name I have been given is Colonel Bradbury, referred to by his friends and contacts as Brad. It is strange that a United States Army officer should be prepared to take money to sell out his own country.

He has been seen drinking with Thai Wong's crowd but it isn't them he is dealing with. Brad visits Thai House Brothel every Tuesday lunch time and he always request the company of a woman there named Bella; she is not connected with him, only in her work. I have had her checked out in depth, just to ensure she is not a go between.

Colonel Bradbury must be a very important link to the gang according to the amount of money he receives. Just one other thing, my friends are undecided if Brad is a minnow, or if he is the kingpin." Rook got up out of the chair said cheerio to Lance and left the office with the 150 American Dollars in his pocket.

Lance put his jacket on and decided to go for a walk around the block to clear his head, which, was pounding, with all the recent revelations he couldn't think straight. He stopped at a small cafe bar and ordered a cognac. He sat enjoying his drink and puffing away at his cigar, suddenly he felt a tap on his shoulder, as he turned around a man said, "My goodness fancy meeting you here Lance." Lance looked up.

"Do I know you?"

"Yes, my name is John Bragg; I was your navigator on several bombing raids"

"I'm sorry John you have the wrong man, I am not a pilot, I work here."

"You have the same scar over your left eye that you came by during a drunken celebration, when we got home on one engine and our plane was badly shot up."

"You are mistaken; excuse me as I have an appointment."

*

Frank was surprised to get a call from John Dawes, the secretary of the local R. A. F. Club. John told him that one of his members is convinced that he met Lance in Berlin but said he had the wrong man. John Bragg had been Lance's navigator on several bombing raids he is so sure it was Lance. It makes the fact, that the Air Ministry took Lance's tunic from us creates a mysterious situation, never mind Frank we will know one day. John Bragg is prepared to gamble that it was Pilot Officer Franks, he is a cigar smoker, cognac drinker, he has the same mannerisms and he has the scar over his left eye, he was present when this happened and he took him to the sick bay to have a stitch put in the cut. As I said Frank, we will know one day as there must be a reason why he doesn't want to be recognized.

Chapter 15

Rook telephoned Lance and it was obvious from the tone of his voice, he was very concerned over something.

"I heard a rumour today that a gang intend smashing their way into the Armoury and steal rifles, machine guns and the ammunition. Apparently, not only does it contain the Allies supplies but also the German Army guns and explosives that had been handed in."

"Rook, is there any substance in this rumour?"

"I don't know. Where is the armoury that is the question?"

"I will make some enquiries and if I am allowed to find out, I will ring you."

Lance was a little uncertain whether or not to pass this rumour on to Max but after some deliberation he decided he should contact him. When he passed the rumour on to Max, he just dismissed it out of hand.

"It's too well guarded by four armed sentries night and day and they been told to shoot anybody trying to gain entry into the building."

"Max, I am glad you have told me this, Rook was very concerned but not enough to ask for money."

Early the following morning Max phoned Lance telling him that it had not just been a rumour. "The attack happened last night. The number of sentries had been reduced to two and they were both stabbed to death, obviously the intruders didn't use gunfire, which would have alerted the army personnel. The intruders had spent several hours selecting the equipment they wanted, rifles, machine guns and several boxes of ammunition to match the guns. Ask Rook to sniff around, if necessary offer him money for any information."

"You told me that you had four soldiers guarding the building?"

"We did have but it was decided that there was little or no threat to the building. It was decided to reduce the cover with two sentries and oddly, it was the first night of the reduced cover. It was a very well planned raid, not only did they spend hours selecting what they wanted, they must have had a shopping list and they used one of the vans to transport the stolen guns away. The van has been found burned out on the Polish Border. I am standing by for the balloon to go up any minute and Brad will have a lot to answer for, it was his decision to reduce the sentries to two, with Brigadier Bolton's approval."

*

As Lance put the phone down it started to ring again. "Hello"

"Hello Lance, This is Rook, you don't have to tell me, I know the armoury was raided last night and there is an arms sale taking place in the small town of Didno in Poland this morning and the most important arms dealers are there. A list of what is for sale is listed on a sales sheet which is being handed to the buyers as they arrive. This was printed before the break- in took place, this indicates how well the operation had been planned. The authorities have issued a statement, saying the weapons are obsolete, don't believe them Lance. The weapons taken are brand new and still in large crates that had never been opened and that applies to the matching ammunition taken. The intruders must have taken a large amount because I am told there are four prominent arms dealers making offers for the weapons and are fighting to get their hands on the guns and believe me we are talking a lot of money. One of my friends phoned and said one dealer from North Korea has made a good offer for the lot, if his offer is accepted, he will organize a plane to fly the crates to Korea within the next hour."

"Rook I have money on the table if you will find out who is selling the arms, this might help us to find out who was behind the break in." Rook rang back.

"Hello Lance, you might be interested to know that both the Brigadier and Colonel Bradbury are there but they don't appear to be involved in any way, we will keep looking. Is it just a coincident they are there?" Lance just smiled to himself.

Gotcha! He sat with a smile on his face; the telephone ringing made him sit up. "Hello"

"Hello Lance, can you spare me five minutes, I would like to speak to you?"

"Yes, can you make at 3.30?"

"Okay, I will see you soon."

I wonder, who the hell have I invited to my office, he smiled, I'll soon find out.

Bang on 3.30 the entry door bell rang, Lance opened the door and an impressive looking gentleman stood on the doorstep.

"Do come in, I am Lance and you are?"

"Hi! Lance, I am Bernie Black and I am the head of the Zionist secret service."

"We have met before Bernie but many moons ago." Lance indicated an armchair for Bernie to sit.

"Would you like a drink?"

"Yes please" Lance left the room and went into a back room, "The young lady will bring our drinks through." As he said that, the young lady came out carrying a tray, on the tray was a pot of tea, a piece of fruit cake and two cognacs, she placed the tray down on the table.

Bernie looked at the tray and studied it, then looked up at Lance and started laughing.

"We have met before, you know my favourite cake?" Lance burst out laughing. "Yes, we met once in London and you insisted on a tray like this one."

"My goodness, I have not been to London for 7 years."

"I was with the British Secret Service when we met." They raised their glasses and toasted each other. "When we have finished our drinks, I will discuss what I have come to speak talk to you about Lance."

"The break- in to the armoury has been on the cards for months, they were just waiting for the crates of new rifles to be delivered. Money changed hands to get the sentries guarding the building to be reduced from four to two. I think it was very sad that those two young soldiers were stabbed to death. I thought the days of violent deaths were behind us now. The people who organized and carried out the raid were Koreans, at this moment in time, I can't tell you if they were from the North or South but whoever they are, they have become desperate for armaments.

After removing the guards, they were at liberty to spend whatever time necessary to select the arms they wanted. There were six of them the man in charge is named Woo-Tin and his brother Ji-Hu and four other people. They identified the crates of new rifles and dragged them and loaded them on to one of the vans. It was a good job there were six of them because the crates are very heavy. I will confirm the names of the two brothers later it might be just a code name they are using to hide their real identity.

When they had the vans loaded, one of the brothers asked the other four to check out the small room, he said there is either gold or money hidden somewhere in that room, if, you find it we will split it six ways. They jumped at the chance. Woo- Tin removed the iron bar from across the solid steel door, when they had entered the room Woo-Tin replaced the iron bar across the door, the four were trapped. There were water bowsers and firefighting equipment around the outside of the building incase of fire from the incendiaries igniting accidently. The bowser outside the building which was a store for Submarine

Batteries had been changed and it now contained sea water. The sea water was pumped through a ventilator on to the batteries, several had been damaged and when the sea water came into contact they started giving off Chlorine gas, which quickly overcame the four Koreans while they were searching for the valuables.

The sea water was switched off and Woo put on a gas mask and checked to make sure all four were dead, when he was satisfied they were dead, he shut the pump down while he removed the pipe from the ventilator and put it down a drain and pumped the sea water down the drains. He opened all the vents and doors in an attempt to clear the evidence of gas.

The two brothers drove the van to the Polish Border where a team was waiting to transfer the arms to another van and set fire to the stolen van. All the known arms dealers had been alerted to attend the small Polish town of Debno the following morning for the sale. I find it difficult to understand why Woo would kill his friends in such a horrible and cruel manner. They were his friends and they helped with the theft of such a valuable haul. Surely there would be enough money to go round. So far North Korea have made the best bid and it looks as if they will purchase the lot, without being blamed for the death of the guards or stealing the arms. Very, Very, Clever."

"Good Lord Bernie, how on earth did you get all this information?"

"Pour me another drink and I will tell you," he said laughing. Lance refilled the glasses.

"I have agents all over the world and I am advised of any threats being planned against any country, particularly my own, which is constantly under threat. In fact, I am not sure about two people who are close to you, Brigadier Bolton and Colonel Bradbury, their names keep cropping up during conversations with my agents. One of my Mossad agents is sure Brad is in constant touch with a gang roaming Poland, what they are looking for we don't know yet?" They shook hands and Bernie left.

Chapter16

Lance sat staring into space when the phone ringing broke his reverie, he picked up the phone and the call was from Bernie. "I have found out why the gangs are roaming around in Poland."

"You had better pop into my office in the morning and tell me all. Will 10am suit you?"

Bernie was on the doorstep when Lance arrived at his office. Lance unlocked the door and they went in and had just sat down when a young lady walked in and went straight into the kitchen to make some coffee but no cognac, it was considered too early in the day.

"The Mossad team, think they have discovered the reason why the gangs are roaming around in Poland and they have also discovered that one member of the gang is on their wanted list. Three of the Spiers family, Otto, Bruno and Rudd were given the job of designing and building the shower units in the Labour camps by Hitler but as you know they were in fact Gas Chambers. The elder brother, Otto, was killed last year by a member of a group calling themselves "Justice Delayed" A list of ten Nazi thugs who had escaped punishment for their part in the atrocities carried out during the German occupation was discovered and a team of international officers killed all of them, one by one. The three brothers arranged the transportation of Jewish families to the labour camps and they proceeded to ransack their houses stealing valuable paintings and silverware. They murdered a Jewish family living in a large house in Poland and have used it for storage for their ill gotten gains.

There will be a lot of opposition but the two remaining Speirs will end up in the gas chamber as did the Jewish people. They were high ranking officers in the Nazi army and their actions were never questioned. Bruno and Rudd know where the goods are stored but will not make a move just yet because too many people are watching and hoping to find the treasure.

Whatever happens the two officers will not live much longer, the high ranking officers of Mossad are being pushed by the victims surviving families to make sure they suffer, as did their parents and grand parents.

Even if the house is found, it will be difficult to return the goods to their rightful owner.

Brigadier Bolton commandeered a beautiful Mercedes car and it is garaged in the area being searched for the treasure. He has stolen a large quantity of top grade Binoculars and they are stored in the boot of the car. He intends having the car crated and shipped to England first and when he returns to the U.S.A. he will take it with him. He feels confident that the customs will turn a blind eye to the home coming forces.

Quite an involved situation Lance but it is difficult to understand how the war years were so wicked."

∗

The girls working in the Thai House made a collective complaint to Lottie stating that the contents of the boxes of supplies have gradually dwindled to half the amount originally promised. Lottie promised to take their complaint to Thai, when she did voice their complaint, he agreed but explained that he was having difficulties in buying the goods on the black market. Lottie, ask them to bear with me and I will make it up to them later. Lottie, I give you my word.

Colonel Bradbury contacted Thai asking for an appointment and a time was agreed. Colonel Bradbury and Brigadier Bolton arrived at Thai's office, when they arrived, Thai asked a young lady to arrange coffee and cognac. "Now gentlemen, how can I help you?"

"You are running a successful and profitable Brothel it must be creating a very good income for you."

"Brigadier, you put the profitable subject in the past tense, for some unknown reason, I can no longer buy the amount of goods on the black market, this is what I pay my girls with, plenty of food for their families, not money."

"Thai, may I remind you that all the territory is under my command and I could shut your operation down but if we can come to some agreement you can continue running the Brothel and I will ensure you receive the necessary supplies. The figure I have in mind for me to receive 50% of your profit."

"I can't pay you 50% it wouldn't be worth my running the operation."

"Okay Thai, I will give you two days to consider my offer. Again, I would point out that I can have you closed down, or arrange for it to continue under new management. Good day Thai, I look forward to hearing from you" and walked out.

Thai dropped into his chair completely stunned.

*

Thai was completely dazed; he wasn't sure what to do or what to think, all his effort, his money and now his operation is being threatened to be taken away from him. He decided to telephone Lance for his thoughts on his problem, he had told Lance all his money making schemes and how legitimate they all are at their last meeting.

Lance invited Thai to call at his office, Thai's tone of voice told Lance that he had a problem. When Thai arrived at Lance's office, it was obvious that he was distraught, he sat down and Lance poured out the coffee and the young lady brought in two cognacs. "Now then Thai, why are you so upset?"

Thai explained how Brigadier Bolton and Colonel Bradbury had visited and insisted he paid them 50% of the Brothels profit, if however, Thai failed to do this, the Brigadier would close the Brothel down or put it under new management, he claims that he has the authority to do this, it is pure blackmail. He knows that I have difficulty in buying supplies on the black market and they are the girl's wages. He claims if I agree, he can supply me with all the supplies I need. How can he direct the supplies here rather than to the warehouse? He has given me two days to consider my position."

"Yes Thai, I too wonder how he can get supplies to sell on the black market. He is in charge of the operation delving into the reason why less arrives at the warehouse that lands and loaded on to the vans. One of his team got killed during an investigation into pilfering of the stock.

Leave this with me Thai, I will enquire; if, in fact he has the authority to do as he claims, I don't think so. Can you arrange for me to receive an inspectors report proving the property and interior is up to standard hygienic conditions and doctor's report on all the girls employed in the building?"

"Yes, I can supply you with this information within an hour; a complete check was carried out two days ago."

"Good, send the copies to my office urgently."

Lance rang London and asked for the name of the person in complete control of the Allied Command in Berlin. Ten minutes later Lance received the call telling him the name was General Francoise Garrard. He telephoned the General's number and managed to get an appointment.

Lance went along to the General's office and he was staggered by the opulence of the office. It had highly polished wooden walls with a decorative desk and a long polished table running the whole length of the room. The furniture was obviously French it was all beautifully inlaid with golden pictures of young ladies gambolling in large grass fields.

The General entered the room, shaking hands he said, "Now then Flying Officer Franks, how can I help you?" Lance was taken aback to be addressed by his rank, which he thought had been buried.

"A brothel has been opened up in the American sector it has been visited and checked by your people to ensure the building is of a high standard. The girls employed as entertainers are checked by the doctors every ten days. In fact, the business is very well regulated and its hygiene is kept to a very high standard." Smiling, Lance said. "It is very popular with the troops to release any sexual urges.

An American Officer has threatened to close down unless the owner pays him 50% of the profit. I would like to enlist your support to keep this operation up and running, here is a recent report." Handing him the reports compiled by the building inspectors and the doctor.

He took the reports from Lance and sat down to read them. "Everything appears to be in order. What can I do to help you?"

"Will you give me a letter authorizing the Brothel to continue and not be closed down by Brigadier Bolton who is trying to blackmail the owner for 50% of the profit?" The General pressed a button and his secretary came into the room. "Rod, I want you to write a letter authorizing the Brothel operation being run by Thai to remain open, as long as long as the present standards are maintained.

When you have typed it, bring the letter in for me to sign, in fact, make it two copies then Lance can have a copy, just to keep everything above board." Smiling as he said it.

*

The following morning Lance visited Thai's office the young lady took him straight through. Lance was appalled when he saw the state of Thai he looked tired, haggard and unkempt. "Thai you look terrible, what is wrong?" The young lady brought in a tray with two coffees.

"Colonel Bradbury called yesterday and told me that he will be taking over the Brothel today. I have sunk all my life's savings into this operation I've even borrowed money depositing the deeds of my home against the loan."

Lance laid one of the letters on Thai's desk, he read it, looked up and he read it again, he leapt to his feet and hugged Lance.

"Would you like to stay here the Brigadier should be here within the next hour?"

"I will wait in the next room and listen, when he realizes he has been defeated, I will come back in this room." They sat down and enjoyed the coffee.

Thai's secretary came into the room to announce that Colonel Bradbury and Brigadier Bolton are here and they would like to see you. Incidentally they have another gentleman with them and are demanding the books and all our records.

Thai smiled, "Show them in to this office." The three gentlemen walked in, the Brigadier looked at Thai and smiled.

"I gave you a very fair offer but you have refused it, I am taking control of this business as from now. Give all your books and records to Gustav and he will take over as chief cashier."

"I am sorry Brigadier but you have no authority to take the business from me."

"Nonsense, I can keep the Brothel up and running or close you down completely."

"Before we go any further, perhaps you would like to read this letter authorized by General Garrard."

The Brigadier read the letter then threw it on the floor. "It is a forgery he would not dare countermand my plans."

His face went red then purple and started shouting and ranting.

"You must leave these premises at once," pulling his revolver from its holster and waving it under Thai's face indicating the door. At this point

Lance entered the room. The Brigadier spun round facing Lance. "Who the hell are you?"

"My name is Lance Franks we have met before, I brought the letter from General Garrard addressed to Thai to enable him to continue his business. In fact, he will be contacting you in a few days to ask from where would you get the supplies to pay the girls and why are you exceeding your authority in a bullying manner?" He put his revolver back in the holster.

Thai smiled. "Would you care for a cup of coffee before you leave?"

Colonel Bradbury just tossed his head and they marched out of the building.

Thai slapped Lance on his back and produced a bottle of cognac out of a cupboard and poured two drinks out. Cheers and they both started laughing nervously.

Chapter 17

Lance was not sleeping too well, at 5 o'clock he got out of bed, put his dressing gown on and went downstairs in to the kitchen. He made himself a cup of coffee and took it into his office Lance picked up a pencil and started doodling on a writing pad. He suddenly became aware of a key being inserted into the lock on the main door, he then heard footsteps. Lance stood behind the door ready to intercept the intruder. He was taken by surprise as Ivan walked in to the room.

"Where on earth have you been Ivan, you have been missing for 10 days?"

"I have been attending several meetings you would not believe the number of Government Officials present, in fact, it appeared to be the whole world was represented. The meeting in general is very concerned the way the World Peace is heading.

I shouldn't discuss with you the main subject but I respect and trust you Lance. The main subject, or should I say the person by the name of Klaus Gunter, he is the scientist who designed and flew the V1's and V2's into Britain the later part of the war. His brain child was creating radio waves to shut down aircraft engines up to the height of 3000 feet. He and his right hand man, Ernst Hahn carried out tests in and outside the laboratory and they were delighted with the result. However the plans and the prototype were stolen out Klaus's steel safe with a secure locking system and it had a secondary lock designed by Klaus himself, it must have been someone very close to know, how and where to blow the locks. It must have been an agent in the pay of a rogue country wanting to get their hands on such a weapon."

*

The main concern voiced, was about the rumour that Klaus had almost perfected a gas to drive an engine, which, can be produced in a laboratory cheaply and the rumour has it that the heat of the engine recycles itself, which, in turn replaces the gas." Lance laughed, "You are now going to tell me what our science master told us about Perpetual Motion."

"You can laugh but all the top brains are very concerned that he may have cracked an age old puzzle."

"The main concern regarding this rumour is the oil producing countries would be devastated and they are prepared to take whatever steps necessary to prevent this happening. Klaus was aware of their anxiety in view of the amount of money offered to stop him experimenting with the gas, which Klaus refused. This is the reason he did not reboard the plane bound for the USA, he didn't die when the aircraft plunged into the Atlantic Ocean. This has been kept a secret but it will be leaked eventually. The people there were quite concerned with the outcome because as you know the economics of the whole world is based on oil."

*

When Klaus decided not to reboard the plane heading to the USA, he went to the railway station and caught a train for Dundee, hoping to trace an old friend of his who had been a prisoner of war and had worked on a farm. When the war finished he decided to remain on the farm where he and the farmer's daughter were married. Han was delighted to find Klaus on his doorstep that was until Klaus told of his scientific experiments and the fact that he was a marked man. "Klaus you can stay here for a couple of days, three at the most. I do not want my house or family involved in your troubles. Klaus, you are too clever for your own good."

"Thanks Han, I will try and arrange transport back to Germany tomorrow I can't wait to join my wife and family again."

The following day Hans told a fellow German of Klaus's visit. He turned to Han,

"That is not possible his plane was brought down to bury his experiments and himself in the Atlantic."

"How do you know this Karl?"

"I have some friends who are desperate for his inventions to be lost."

"Believe me or not, just pop in this evening and meet him."

"Han, be very careful. There are some very rich and powerful people trying to prevent Klaus's gas propulsion system being incorporated into the average family car. Just think how it would affect the oil producing countries economies. I can tell you that they will not allow anything or person to put their economies at risk."

Karl did visit Han and his family that evening to make sure it was Klaus that Han was talking about. He was made very welcome and after speaking to Klaus he was convinced Klaus, was who Han said he was. After two hours of chatting and enjoying a glass of wine he decided to leave to go home. On arriving home he immediately made a phone call to a friend knowing he would be well paid for passing on this information.

*

Lance sat in his office going through some old papers, looking for what he wasn't sure. The phone rang, when he picked up the receiver the caller sounded a little panic stricken. "This is Rook can I come round, it is urgent?"

"Yes come round, the side door is open."

Ten minutes later Rook walked into Lance's office.

"What is so urgent Rook?"

"The oil producing countries have formed a consortium and have bought a large house on the outskirks of Berlin which, they are converting into flats and they are building an extensive laboratory at the back of the house. It is whispered that they have Klaus in mind. They are confident they will obtain the formula, they must have some plan in mind of how to persuade Klaus to part with it."

"Thanks Rooks, I will put this info into the pot and see what comes out."

Lance mind started ticking over, can we make some money with this info.

He rang Max and told him a little of Rook had told him.

"Lance whatever it costs get me the full account of what is in the mind of the consortium and why Klaus? You know I am now allowed to spend to keep up to date with other powers. Why Klaus, I thought he was killed in the air crash?"

"No Max, he wasn't killed, he is in Scotland and is trying to get a lift back to Germany."

"Thanks Lance."

Max telephoned the officer in charge of the American Airbase in Scotland asking him to make it known that they are prepared to give Klaus a seat on an aircraft destine for Germany.

Klaus went to an American Base to enquire if he could possibly obtain a lift to Germany he was given a chair to sit down while the girl in the reception enquired, he was astounded at the treatment he received. Several minutes later an officer came into the room, shaking hands, he told Klaus that they will give him a lift in two days time. Klaus always regarded himself as a tough guy but on this occasion he had a job to stop tears from rolling down his face.

When Klaus told Han of his plans, Han's face gave away the relief he felt knowing that Klaus was leaving his house. Karl's interest in Klaus made Han nervous. On the third morning Klaus left the house early and Han gave him a lift to the Airbase on his way to work.

Arriving at the base he was given a mug of coffee and taken out to the aircraft he would be flying in. The seats were obviously a portable affair but Klaus found the seat very comfortable and the plane was carrying about thirty people. He felt very comfortable with the thought of going home. He stretched out his legs, this is bliss, the engines fired up and they started rolling and he was delighted when the aircraft left the ground. He suddenly felt the urge to visit to the toilet, when he returned he found that his seat had been taken but there were several seats available so he sat three rows back. The flight was a comfortable one and the landing was as it would come out of the flying textbook. The man who had taken Klaus's seat did not move, on inspection the stewardess found that he had been stabbed with a long blade from the back of the seat and the man was dead. Klaus was devastated he realized the blade was intended for him.

Chapter 18

Klaus was given a lift to his home address he was so excited to be home to see his wife and two daughters. He opened his garden gate and fumbled for his door key, opened the door and stepped into the hallway, as he stepped in he was jumped on by two burly men and they dragged him into the lounge. His wife and two daughters were sat on the settee surrounded by four big black shaven headed men, one had a bushy ginger beard and another had a long black beard, very frightening. They were at least six feet six inches tall and heavily built, the man who was obviously in charge had a mouthful of gold teeth in fact, he was very intimidating. His wife's face was deathly white and the girls were both sobbing.

"Klaus we have called for the formula of your invention for gas production to propel a rocket or it can be adapted for family car engines. We do not intend any harm but we will not leave without it."

"I'm not prepared to give it to you it consists of my three years work." Without saying anything, one of the men pulled Klaus's wife to her feet and ripped her blouse and bra off. She being a big lady she was very conscious of her large floppy breasts and tried to hide them with her hands but the man behind her, put his arms round her and squeezed her breasts, she spun around and slapped his face. He turned her round and hit her with the back of his hand which sent her sprawling across the floor.

Klaus went to get up to protect her but he was pushed back into his seat.

"Klaus, you can see we intend to get your formula. Will you give it to us now?"

His wife shook her head side to side, indicating no.

"You still refuse to give me the formula?"

One of the gorillas stood the elder daughter to her feet and they slowly undressed her down to her panties.

Still Klaus refused to part with his papers.

The men proceeded to completely strip his wife of her clothes, she stood completely naked and she still shook her head. For several minutes his wife was made to stand in front of them naked and they walked round her and she had the indignity of having to listen to the men's lewd comments.

The younger daughter was the next target, again they slowly removed all her clothing and one of the gorillas dragged her in front her parents, he held her with his left arm over her left shoulder and squeezed her left nipple and this made her whimper, at the same time taking her right hand in his to rub his enlarged crotch.

When Klaus still refused, the gorilla nodded to two of the men to hold the girl with her legs parted. She was screaming "Stop them Daddy" Klaus made no move but when he saw the gorilla drop his trousers, his appendage was the size he had never seen been before.

"Stop, you can have the papers" but they had difficulty in stopping the gorilla advancing on the girl. "Allow my wife and the girls to dress and regain some dignity and I will get the papers you want." The mother and daughters dressed themselves.

Klaus walked to the corner of the room, lifted the corner of a large rug and lifted a small area of the floor boards and lifted out the large folder, handed it to the leader. "If it isn't the formula, we will be back."

"That folder contains three years of my life." The six men walked out of the door leaving it open.

They sat in a family huddle crying and whimpering. It had been a terrifying experience for the parents and the young girls.

"I am so sorry you had to give up all the years of work Klaus." Klaus looked at his wife smiled and winked his right eye. "They will get more than they bargained for when they follow the writings in the formula, they violated my precious family."

"You haven't Klaus?"

"Yes Flora I have."

Rook contacted Lance telling him that Klaus was back in Berlin and there were all sorts of rumours flying around. A North Korea group claims to have got the formula and with all the stolen arms they bought, they claim to be invincible and they have started a war of words with the South.

Lance received a message that Bernie would like to meet him, he phoned Bernie and arranged to meet him for coffee the following morning at 10.30. The café bar was quite close to Lance's office, as he approached the bar he could see Bernie sat enjoying his cognac. Bernie rose from his chair to shake hands with Lance. Bernie looked at Lance with usual mannerism, his head leaning to his left shoulder. "Have you any news of the Klaus saga?"

"No, the only news I have been given over the past few days is that a group of the oil producing countries have formed a consortium, to take the necessary steps to prevent Klaus's gas invention threatening their oil revenues and they will stop at nothing to get hold of the formula. They have bought a large house on the outskirts of the city and they are having, or had a large laboratory built on the same grounds. The house is being converted into apartments obviously to house the scientists."

"Lance, I have been told that Klaus was flown back to Berlin in an American aircraft several days ago."

"That will have been Max's doing"

"Rumour also has it that Klaus was persuaded to hand over the formula, I have yet to find out if it is true, if it is, I wonder how they persuaded him, he turned down a large cash inducement to hand it over by the same North Koreans who bought the stolen arms."

They sat quietly enjoying the sunshine when they heard a terrific explosion it even vibrated their cups and saucers on the table. All sorts of tales started to be passed around until a policeman told them that a large house on the outskirts and the adjoining laboratory had both been reduced to a heap of rubble. They looked at each other and just smiled.

Lance and Bernie were so engrossed in discussing the world situation in general that they were not aware that a man was standing behind them until he said. "Good morning gentlemen."

They were startled, looking down, the man said, "You are Bernie, yes?"

"Yes I am but although we have met before but I can't remember where or who you are."

"My name is Klaus Gunter and we did meet in Liverpool quite a few years ago"

Lance stood up and dragged another chair to the table, "Please join us" and he ordered another coffee. Bernie looked at him. "We have heard so many stories about you. First you died in an aircraft crash, then the tale goes that you took the money for your invention and moved to a warmer climate."

"May we move to another table away from all the flapping ears?"

"Certainly" and they moved to a small table farther away from the other diners.

"The day before I left Scotland on a USAF plane, I was sat having a coffee as we are today when a man came and sat beside me, he did mumble an introduction of himself. When you go back to Berlin, look up Lance Franks and enlist his help as you are a marked man, which is now, looking at Lance. The man told me that he was a British Intelligence agent and on my return I was to protect my back from two people. The names are not known but they are both US Army officers, one is a Brigadier and the other is either a Captain or a Lieutenant."

Bernie looked at Lance and smiled.

*

"An Asian group claim to have your formula, they said that you were persuaded to hand it over to them Klaus, is this true?"

"I trust you and Bernie, I will tell you the truth but you must respect my confidence." Lance looked at Klaus. "If you want us to listen but not to repeat, you have it Klaus." Bernie and Lance looked up at Klaus expectantly, Klaus started telling his story. "When I arrived home and entered the front door I was dragged into the lounge, there were six coloured gentlemen, they stood at least six feet six inches tall and very muscular and heavily built. One had a ginger bushy beard and another had long black beard, they looked very intimidating and they were all shaven headed. I thought we had been invaded by gorillas, they were vicious. They asked for my formula but I refused to part with it. They violated my wife and when I still refused they chose my elder daughter, when I still refused they stripped my younger daughter and prepared to rape her, I could not sit and watch such a thing happen to my little girl and she was screaming to me to stop them. It was then I gave way and handed them the formula.

They would not be aware how volatile the gas is without the inducement of the calming gas. During the early experiments we had several small explosions until I learned how to add a calming gas, which enabled it to be worked with."

"Is that the reason for the explosion that destroyed the house and the laboratory?"

Klaus smiled, "Yes and I hope the six gorillas were in the building and perished."

"That is harsh Klaus."

"Not if you had to sit and watch the disgusting way they treated your family, as I did."

"Nice to have met you again Bernie and I hope we shall meet again Lance I will bear in mind what your friend said." Klaus walked off.

Chapter 19

It was such a beautiful day Klaus decided to stroll down to the canal and enjoy a walk along the towpath, he felt at peace with the world the happiest he had felt for months but he didn't realize he was being followed. He was walking past a large number of houseboats, some were a good condition but the majority was in a dreadful state of repair, many had been knocked together by groups of families to provide accommodation for their own family as they had lost their house and all their possessions during bombing raids during the war. This was the best they could do until they got back on their feet again.

He was half way down the long line of boats when two heavily built men grabbed him and pushed him aboard an old dilapidated houseboat and kicked him down the steps into the cabin. The two men followed him into the cabin and tied him to a chair and gagged him to keep him quiet.

Klaus had been missing for two days, his wife notified the authorities they took all her details and promised to investigate. Arriving home, she had a look in his desk and found a note saying, that if he should be involved in any problem contact Lance and there was a phone number. She phoned Lance telling him that Klaus had been missing for two days.

"How did you get my phone number Mrs. Gunter?"

"Klaus had left it on a pad by the phone apparently a British Agent told him to do this."

"Thanks for ringing Mrs. Gunter, I will do my best to find him, try not to worry."

As soon as Lance put the phone back down on the cradle, it started to ring again, he picked the instrument up. "Hello Lance, this is Rook, it is rumoured that Klaus has been kidnapped and is being held hostage on a houseboat near a bridge on the canal."

"Rook, there are twenty seven bridges in Berlin, in fact we have more bridges here than in Venice, which one?"

"I will try and find out."

Lance next received a call from Bernie. "A fine state of affairs Lance, have you any idea where Klaus is being kept?"

"No, the only information I have at present is that he is being held hostage on a houseboat near a bridge. Not much to go on but must find him before he is killed."

"One of my agents attached a tracer on Brad and the Brigadiers car hoping it will lead us to the boat. Hang on a moment Lance."

"They have a trace from Brad's car but it is in the car park near the canal not to a specific boat, it is going to be difficult as there are so many boats, some are just heaps of rubbish and bear no resemblance of a boat." Agent Manny went to the car park and followed Brad as he walked along the towpath. Brad stopped to speak to a man who was going through the motions of painting his boat he was using brush strokes but not dipping his bush into a paint pot, for some reason he had no paint on his brush, obviously a lookout. Brad boarded a boat on pier 73 but there were five boats tied up alongside each other so he isn't sure which boat Brad went into. Two more agents joined Manny to watch the towpath, after ten minutes Brad stepped off pier 74 he must have jumped across as they are all closely moored. One of the agents followed him while Manny still watched the boats as his leaving could be a red herring. The agent who followed Brad was surprised to follow him to Brad's home address, the picture fell into place half an hour later as the Brigadier's car pulled up and he entered Brads home. Lance, I am convinced they are up to something."

Two mossad agents kept a constant vigil on the piers 70-74 and they were soon rewarded, two men boarded the third boat out and disappeared down into the cabin, after about five minutes two different men came up from the cabin and left the row of boats and stepped on to the towpath, obviously it was a changeover of the watch.

Bernie discussed the situation with Lance and they decided to investigate the crew on boat number three in the early hours of the following morning. Before the planned time to board the boat, one of Bernie's agents reported that Brad's car had entered the car park and Brad had boarded one of the boats. Lance became a little concerned whether or not to call for back up to prevent a confrontation and the possibility of gunfire. Bernie called upon two more of his agents and Lance called for two British Secret Service agents to join him.

It was decided that they would board the boat at 1.30 in the morning. When they met up, the weather was atrocious, snowing and bitterly cold. They boarded the boat, Bernie and his two men were to enter the cabin and Lance and his agents were to cover their backs.

As Bernie stepped down the ladder he could not see anyone then suddenly a man jumped up and became face to face with Bernie, one of Bernie's men chopped the man on his neck with the side of his hand, the man fell to the floor with a broken neck his fall was caught to prevent any noise.

They crept quietly into the cabin and they could see a man sat at a table drinking coffee with an automatic rifle laid on the table and two men each tied to a chair and gagged. One was Klaus but the other they did not recognize he had oriental features. The mossad agent took no chances, he quietly crept behind the man drinking coffee and ran his knife across his throat and he crumbled without a sound.

They released the two men in the chairs, one was Klaus and when Lance came aboard he identified the other man a Thai, who was extremely pleased it was Lance involved in the rescue. Lance looked at Thai, "Why you?"

"They thought I was in your team the way you dealt with the Brothel problem."

One of Bernie's agents dashed aboard telling him that the two tagged cars had arrived in the car park and several men are walking towards the boats. They decided to extinguish all the lights except a low glow bulb in the lower cabin. They heard footsteps, as they stepped on the boat they could feel a rocking movement of the boat on the water. The intruders came down the ladder and when they saw the empty chairs Brad shouted, "Otto! What the hell is going on?"

Lance and Bernie stepped out of the shadow to face the Brigadier and Brad. The Brigadier shouted "You" He pulled out his revolver and shot Bernie then Lance and hurriedly left the scene. One of Bernie's crew called an ambulance and Bernie and Lance were taken off to hospital. The man who had taxied Lance in the jeep to meet Max was sat on a form on the towpath and he witnessed what had happened. He telephoned Max and told him what had taken place but he did not say which young lady he was sat with on the form when he witnessed the incident. Fortunately, neither were badly injured, Bernie had been shot in the thigh and Lance had been shot in the shoulder and was bleeding profusely and the ambulance man concentrated on stemming the flow of blood.

*

Max visited Lance in hospital to confirm that it was the Brigadier who shot him. I will have to get an officer of the same or of a higher rank to arrest him and remand him in the cells of the guard room.

When the Brigadier was confronted and was told he was being arrested and charged with the shooting of a British Secret Service Agent and Israeli Senior Mossad officer. "I shot them because they are being funded by an enemy country."

"Nonsense, it is your second in command, Lieutenant Bradbury who is in the pay of the enemy, he receives a monthly payment direct into his bank from a Russian source." Brad was accused of being a double agent at his court- martial in fact the judge said he was a spy, which Brad strongly denied. After listening to the arguments for and against the case, the five officers rose from their seats and retired to an adjoining room.

The room was called to attention and the five officers returned to their seats and Brad was called back into the room to face them. The senior officer of the board addressed Brad. "Lieutenant Bradbury, we had listened and considered all the arguments put forward but we have made a unanimous decision that you are guilty as charged of being a spy and will face a firing squad to be shot dead."

Brad broke down and fell to the floor he had to be virtually carried out of the room.

When Brad had regained his composure, he asked to speak to a senior officer. An officer came into the cell and sat down. "What do you want to discuss?" Brad looked at the officer, "If I passed you some very important information, can we do a deal?"

"Have we a deal or not?"

"I will have to discuss your request with the Judges who conducted the court-martial and the legal teams" Fifteen minutes later the officer returned accompanied with two of the senior officers. One of the officers faced Brad saying, "It all depends on what information you are prepared to pass to us. Whatever you tell us will be thoroughly checked before a decision is made and what you want is the sentence to be shot commuted to a prison sentence, is that correct?" Brad just nodded his head.

Brad explained about the contents of a large house in Poland, in this house are valuable paintings, furniture, gold and silver all stored from the plundering of many Jewish properties. "Where is this house that you claim to be Aladdin's Cave?"

Brad gave them the Polish house address.

"This address will be checked out before we make a decision" They all left the room locking the door behind them. Brad sat hoping against hope that the Brigadier has not got there first and removed the valuable items. He was placed in a cell and left overnight but he had very little sleep dreading the thought of being taken out the next morning to be shot. He being an American serviceman, the President of America must confirm the sentence.

*

The Brigadier refused to recognize the authority of the people arresting him as they were not senior to his rank. He did convince them enough to allow him to remain in his own quarters under house arrest. The second night when darkness had fallen, he slipped out of his quarters undetected and made his way to the house in Poland using a jeep from the motor pool. He quietly entered the house and collected the small valuable hand painted icons of the Tsar's Russian family and put them together by the front door. He went into the garage to collect his beautiful Mercedes car he had to fire the engine several times before it would start and run smoothly. He decided to change into the civilian clothes that he had left in the car just in case of a situation as this. Things had not worked out as he had planned and now he was a little undecided which way to go.

Chapter 20

Brad was taken into the interrogation room and he was told that they had recovered quite a number of valuable paintings but not the amount he had told them existed. Having recovered these items your future is being discussed by the senior officers of the court.

"The house was searched and it appears the owners were taken to a labour camp and no one has heard of them since. We should learn later if our Commander is prepared to do a deal on the strength of what they found. If you should get a prison sentence it should be a light one in view of your war service."

"The fact is that you received a monthly income from a Russian source paid directly into your bank in America this is quite damning evidence to your case."

"The money is going into my bank account but I have to pay the Brigadier 50% of that money, in cash. The Brigadier has complete control over me I have to do exactly as he says. One of my family was taken ill in America and required specialist treatment which we could not afford but as I was in charge of the fiancés in the catering department dealing with the wines, I fiddled the accounts and paid for my small boys operation. He discovered the cash shortage and threatened to expose me and I would be dishonorably discharged, I would lose my pension, which is due in four years time. He has a hold over several other officers who are in the same position as I, completely at his beck and call. The Brigadier is the Mr. Big in Berlin, shall we call by his proper name, Horace. He controls several gangs in the city he is responsible for a third of the goods flown in disappearing which ends up on the streets as Black Market goods. The guns and ammunition stolen from the armory was of his doing. He has made a lot of money selling some of them but he still has a fair quantity still looking for a buyer. He pays the leaders of his gangs handsomely, he is buying loyalty.

I should speak to Lance Franks and Bernie Black as they are on his hit list, I am not fantasizing he has issued a list of people he wants to disappear. Klaus Gunter is also on the list as the consortium wants his experiments stopped and they are offering a fantastic sum of money to make sure this in done.

*

Horace jumped into his car but he was undecided which way to go, he would have difficulty in avoiding his enemies and hopefully get to the coast and scrounge a lift to England, once there, he can get home to the USA with this beautiful Mercedes. He sat pondering shall I turn right or left? He joined the main carriageway and he was flagged down to stop by a U.S officer who had brought all the traffic to a halt to allow an army convoy of US lorries, jeeps and tank carrying vehicles to pass. When the convoy had passed, Horace decided to go in their direction and catch up with them, which he did after motoring forty five minutes. When he came along side the convoy he could see they had stopped to serve food, he changed back into his Brigadiers uniform and strolled up to the kitchen. He was immediately offered food and another officer gave him a beer, which he accepted gratefully.

The officer told him that they all had their bed rolls with them and they were staying put for the night. One of the lorries had broken down and it was decided to leave it behind as the engine had blown up and was beyond repair on the road. Horace went back to his car and managed to find tools he removed the number plates from the lorry and put them on his car. It won't fool the authorities completely but long enough to give him space. The following morning several of the drivers were fooling around and one of them stepped back, the noise made metal on metal, the soldier looked down and saw the number plates on the ground. He picked them up, looked at them and then threw them over the hedge into an overgrown field. Horace felt sure they would have heard his sigh of relief. While having a beer with an officer the previous evening he learned that the convoy was on route to Calais, there they would board a ferry and take the vehicles and equipment to England and then at a later date taken on to the USA.

*

Several days later after having several hiccups with the vehicles, they finally arrived at the port of Calais late one afternoon. The kitchen was set up and food was made available to the drivers and they were told that they would be sleeping on their bed rolls inside their vehicles. The officer in charge emphasized, that they must protect their goods and food from roaming gangs scavenging for food or vehicle parts. The following morning they were herded together and the long tank carrying vehicles were taken aboard first and loading took place according to size. When Horace was in positioned on the ferry, he got out, locked the car and made his way to the top deck. He couldn't believe his good fortune. Bernie had been alerted that the Brigadier had absconded and he was put under pressure to trace him. The senior members of Mossad have discovered that he had been responsible for five Jewish families being taken to a labour camp and put in the shower unit and their property plundered. They are determined that he too will be placed in one of these shower units rather than be assassinated by shooting. Bernie decided to send a team to England to watch the docks as the forces were disembarking and four were on the same ferry as Horace.

When the agents had finished eating they decided to have a look around the ferry's hold. One of the agents reported back and told the leader that he had found a suspicious vehicle it was a car carrying army number plates which doesn't match. The leader went with him to investigate and when really studied the car the leader said "Gotcha." The plan was laid for when they arrived at Dover.

They kept a careful eye on Horace's movements and when arrived in Dover and the ferry was safely moored the vehicles started to leave the boat. The Brigadier got into his car and joined the queue to leave the ferry, he went down the ramp on to the docks and they asked him, if he had any contraband on board the car. He shook his head indicating no but the man insisted that he got out of the car. Which, he most reluctantly did, as he put his feet to the floor three heavily built men hustled him to the floor, they lifted him to his feet and covered his uniform with a long black cloak, put him in a car that was parked on the dockside and driven off. One of the agents drove the Mercedes off the dock area into a secure building to be searched

*

Bernie received the message that Brigadier Bolton was under arrest, he immediately passed the message on Lance but he was upset to be controlling operations from a hospital bed. They are both hoping to be discharged in a couple of days, Ivan joked with Lance saying he was just skiving and he liked the attention of the pretty nurses. Bernie told his team to take Horace back to Berlin and make sure he is kept under arrest. In spite of all the Brigadiers arrogance and protests they took him on board the returning ferry as instructed. When the ferry arrived in Calais a car was waiting to take him to a safe place to be interrogated by the Mossad team.

Chapter 21

Rook telephoned Lance telling him that a rumour is going around that the Russians have not given up on transporting the machinery and the machine tools to Russia. The machinery had been left at the airport and it had been sprayed with a light, lubricating oil and covered over with an oiled tarpaulin, hoping this will prevent rust attacking any part of the machinery or the tools.

"A team of German engineers has been assembled to go to the airport and dismantle the machinery into manageable parts bearing in mind the weight that can be handled, using a mobile crane to lift the parts on to a low loader and transported to a seaport. The seaport being talked about is Bremerhaven which is the nearest port which has the facilities, such as overhead cranes and it has access to the North Sea. The officials are also happy with that area as the Russian Navy is present in force. Lance, if I relate all to you can we talk money later, I was there during the final stages."

"Yes Rook, just tell me all you have."

"The machinery and the machine tools were loaded without a hitch and it was sheeted and was secured, firstly it was covered with a sheet then roped and blocks were used to prevent the machinery from moving. You can tell how nervous they were, every few minutes they kept checking the ropes then the blocks, if it had not been so serious it could have been laughable."

Several Russian officers were wandering around and were very vigilant hoping to prevent a chaos as before. Several of the officers started to check the wheels and tires until a senior officer came and told them that there were ten wheels as used on aircraft, solid rubber on a slim rim, these were being used in view of the weight and it is hoped they will survive the 200 mile journey to the Port. One of the officers was very concerned about the smug look on the faces of the German engineers, a look of defiance.

The officers made a final check and then the wagon started off heading in the direction of Bremerhaven, the officers all breathed a sigh of relief.

Ron Walters

The officers and their men escorting the convoy were congratulating themselves as everything appeared to be going swimmingly and they were ten miles into the journey. Suddenly there was an explosion, one of the rubber tires was in shreds and the wheel was just running on the rim. The officer in charge contacted the nearest depot which was in Zehiendorf asking for a replacement wheel, as the message filtered out to the German engineers who were standing around in groups, they all started cheering, laughing and jeering at the Russians. The officer in charge of the depot selected six of the engineers to go with the lorry taking the wheel to the stricken wagon but when they arrived they were faced with the prospect of lifting the trailer to replace the wheel. The weight was beyond the capabilities of the jacks they have in the tool kit. It was decided to wait for a mobile crane or some other vehicle capable to lift such a weight. The officer in charge was frantic, thinking they might have to unload to reduce the weight. After a wait of one hour a mobile crane turned up with various attachments for lifting vehicles. They got cracking and after half an hour they were mobile and ready to move on, much to the senior officer's relief. The lorry left taking the German engineers back to the depot with it. The convoy was supposed to stop for refreshment stop after 22 miles but in view of the hold up the officer cancelled this arrangement and made his men to keep going as he knew they had a deadline to achieve. The ship they were to meet, load and take the machinery to Russia was at the mercy of the tides, therefore the convoy must keep going.

The officer did relent a little, he sent two men ahead to arrange for them to collect food and drink, pass it round but keep going. His men were far from happy with the arrangements as they had been working hard over the past week and were very tired.

The officers were pleased with themselves, they had a hiccup but they have made up the time they lost with the wheel problem. They checked and they found that they had covered just over one hundred miles, so, they were half way to the port. They had just finished patting each other on the back when there was another explosion, this time it was a rear wheel that exploded and again it was impossible to continue without a rubber tyre. The senior officer was frantic, what shall we do now? He had no option but to contact the local depot in Hanover, they in turn

132

contacted a vehicle depot near to them but they were unable to supply a wheel or the tyre necessary to continue the journey. Arrangements was made for them to spend the night in a local barrack and hoped their own depot could arrange a wheel for the morning and the local people supply the lifting gear. The local commandant wanted the incident investigating as the tyres should not disintegrate and it became obvious the convoy would not reach the port in time to be loaded and the ship to catch the tide as planned.

"The convoy arrived two hours too late, the ship sailed on the arranged tide. The machinery has been left on the dockside covered to protect it from the weather but two of the rubber tyres were in shreds it was so obvious that the Germans did not want to see their future being taken away. The problem the Russians are faced with now is to wait for a ship that has a shallow draught suitable for the harbour in Bremerhaven. A Russian warship is moored just outside the harbour to ensure that a rogue ship doesn't slip into the harbour load the machinery and sail off."

"Rook, I can tell you exactly what happened but remember I'm telling you this in confidence. A small hole had been drilled into the solid tyre and a small cylinder containing explosive material inserted. With the weight of the machinery and the friction of the tyres on the road this had created heat and after the vehicle had travelled a number of miles the heat became intense, it activated the explosive material to an unstable condition causing it to explode."

"How do you know this Lance?"

Lance just smiled and touched the side of his nose.

Chapter 22

Bernie called at Lance's office and knocked on the door, Lance opened the door. "Hello Bernie, it's great to see you, hope you keeping well?"

"I have come with cap in hand asking for your help."

"Bernie, I know we are friends but what makes you think I can help you?"

"I spoke to a colleague in London and he pointed me in your direction and he thought Colonel Snaith might also help. Who is this man Lance?"

"All I am at liberty to tell you is, his office is in Whitehall, London and he controls the British Secret Service."

"Thanks Lance."

Lance started laughing. "Cup of coffee first, is it too early for your cognac?"

"No it will help my brain to start ticking over." Lance made the coffee and placed the cognac in front of Bernie.

"Now Bernie how can I help you?"

"The mossad council have put me under pressure to find the two remaining Spiers brothers Rudd and Bruno, the third brother Otto, was killed by the group calling themselves "Justice Delayed" I am a little surprised they missed the other two because as you know they built the gas chambers under the a guise by calling them Shower Units. They were responsible for transporting Jewish families to the so called labour camps and they were never seen or heard of again. When they had transported the families they systematically stole anything of value in the houses and stored it all in a large house in Poland.

The relatives of the families are clamouring to have them arrested and face the same suffering and end as their families did, by gassing, they were and still are listed as Nazi murdering thugs.

One of the hand painted icons which has now been stolen by the Brigadier was in fact painted by my grandfather and it is a painting of my own family when I was very young. I would like to recover it whatever money it would cost.

I sent one my senior agents to the outskirts of Berlin as I was told Rudd had been spotted in that area and I have heard that the agent named Gordon has located Rudd and he would keep in touch."

*

Gordon spent several days just wandering the streets hoping he would be lucky to spot Rudd, it was this area that he had been seen before. He went into a café bar, he couldn't believe his eyes, there was Rudd sat on a bar stool drinking a cup of coffee. Rudd finished his drink and shouted to his friends before leaving, Gordon got up from his chair and followed him, hoping he will lead him to his home address. The café bar was below a large block of flats, Gordon followed Rudd into the building and along a long corridor, he saw Rudd turn right down a passage way, he followed. Twenty yards down the passage way he was jumped on and wrestled to the ground, picked up and taken into an adjacent flat. He was pushed into a chair, Rudd pulled up a chair facing Gordon staring at him with dark beady eyes through metal rimmed glasses.

"You are Gordon Tinsley and your boss is Bernie Black, it appears you are looking for me, why?"

"I have no idea, I was to find you and pass the information back to Bernie."

"You can tell Bernie Black that if he sends any more of his agents here, they will be dealt with, we had intended killing you but we have changed our mind and make you the messenger boy. Remember to tell him to stay away from me and my friends, you may leave now." Looking across at two men who had been leaning on the bar and had bundled Gordon into the room, he just nodded.

Gordon sighed deeply as he left the building but he didn't realize that he was being followed by two men. The men suddenly rushed at him and pushed him into the undergrowth which was bordering the road. When they got Gordon in the long grass and small trees they started punching him to the floor, as he laid there they kicked and hit him with a baseball bat. This went on for some time and they ran off. Gordon was lying on the grass covered in blood and with many broken bones, how many he will not know until he is checked over. Bernie phoned Lance telling him that Gordon had not called in and no one has had contact.

"I will ask around Bernie, Rook might hear some street gossip." The next person Lance phoned was Max and explained how concerned Bernie has become.

"The only man who resembles Gordon is a man found battered and was taken to hospital suffering from a broken leg, 3broken ribs, 2 broken fingers and deep cuts and bruising to his face."

"My goodness, the poor man has really been battered and is very lucky to be still alive."

Bernie visited the hospital hoping against hope that it isn't Gordon who has been found more dead than alive. As he entered the ward he was met with a shocking sight, it was Gordon lying in the bed, his leg in a sling, wires attached to his chest and an oxygen mask on his face held in place with an elastic strap.

*

Rook phoned Lance telling him that he had heard about Gordon being badly beaten. Rudd and Bruno are among friends at least they are regarded as friends but they are a group of men of mixed ages. They have hired a room at the back of a Bar and they parade in the hall several times each week dressed in full Nazi SS Uniforms even down to the highly polished black leather Jack Boots. They have let it be known that they will protect Rudd and Bruno as they are regarded as heroes for removing the threat of Jews. Lance this is a serious matter and it is likely to gain momentum. Investigating deeper Lance found that this group has a special section imitating a shrine in the hut devoted to Otto who was killed in Brazil whilst diving. The coroners findings was that his tank run out of oxygen but this was not the case, a member of the Mossad team had tampered with his breathing apparatus which caused him to die of suffocation as he went very deep. Killed by a Jew whose family who had too, died from suffocation in Otto's gas chamber. Lance telephoned Bernie and told him exactly what Rook had passed on and Lance could tell by Bernie's voice this information had come as a shock.

"Lance I had been told that it was a uniformed couple who carried out the attack on Gordon using baseball bats, until now, I had dismissed this witness's statement but now with what you have told me, it could have been the case."

"Bernie, I am sorry to hear this."

"Good God Lance, I hope we are not seeing anti Semitism raising its ugly head again. I was in Brazil at the time of Otto's death, your Home Secretary had sent two men out to Brazil to create a dossier on Otto but he was dealt with without their help. Perhaps I shouldn't tell you but I will, he was a member of the group "Justice Delayed" and he had drawn the short straw to deal with Otto."

*

Lance decided that in view of the deteriorating situation some action was necessary to come up with a plan to stop the younger generation getting involved with anti Semitism starting up again. It was decided to hold the meeting in Lance's office, there were four of them, Ivan, Lance, Bernie and the local Jewish Rabbi. Bernie and Lance suggested that two young Jewish boys should walk past the Nazi sympathizers hall, should they be attacked we will on an outer ring to deal with the attackers.

Ivan looked up, "This will be provocation you are just looking for trouble."

"No Ivan we just want to stop these people thinking they can do as they like to the Jews and get away with it, times have changed."

"You may be right Lance but I have seen so much violence over the past few years and I am just fed up with mankind being so bitter with his neighbour."

"Ivan if you don't agree, we respect your feelings and will not ask or expect you to take part."

Lance suggested they took a vote whether or not they try the plan out, which, they did and three out of the four decided to go ahead with the plan.

A watch was kept on the café bar and it became apparent that a Thursday night is when they all muster in the hall. It was arranged to carry out the plan the following Thursday, there was no need to ask for support from the local Jewish community, Lance was surprised with number of people wanting to take part but Bernie read the riot act, they must not be too violent. The object of the exercise is to demonstrate that the Jews are no longer going to be pushed around. We are German citizens and we pay our taxes, therefore we to deserve respect. If they do attack the two boys we will make sure they are aware our feelings.

On the Thursday evening there several stragglers going to the hall and it was quite obvious they saw the two boys walking down the road which would take them past the hall. A few minutes went past when several of the of the boys dressed in the full SS Nazi uniform came out of the hall and approached the two boys, one of the uniformed youth tapped one of the Jewish boys on his back and the others went to join into the attack but the team of Jewish men stepped in and proceeded to give the boys a pasting and they took the baseball bats and their armbands displaying the Nazi emblem away from them, they ran off back to the hall.

Bernie and his team got together and they all hoped that this will nip the nastiness in the bud.

Chapter 23

Klaus contacted Lance asking for an appointment. "I have made a decision and I want to discuss my plan with you as I value your opinion."

"Okay Klaus call round this afternoon about 3 o'clock, I am intrigued and I am looking forward to hear your plan and what it entails."

Klaus rang Lance's doorbell bang on 3o'clock. Lance opened the door and Klaus entered and they sat down on the settee, Lance had the coffee ready.

"Right Klaus, what is your plan and I will be truthful in my reply?" Klaus smiled.

"I will invite all the prominent international scientists from around the world to attend a lecture to be delivered by myself and I intend to have all my papers copied. Each person present will receive a copy covering all the aspects of my years of work.

Any country will have the ability to call up any of my inventions, instead of a rogue country gaining the advantage over his neighbour.

As you know I boarded the plane destine for the States together with my team and their families but when we landed in Scotland I decided not to reboard the plane because my family had refused to go with me and I realized I couldn't leave them. I visited a friend of mine in Dundee and it was Max who arranged for me to get a seat on a USAF plane to return to Berlin.

The tragedy of the plane crashing in the Atlantic was a sad affair. The instrument that was on board the plane, when activated it would shut down the engines, which is exactly what happened. This instrument had been stolen from my safe and it appears to have been on its way to America. Who stole it or who activated it I have no idea but it was intended to kill me.

On the way home in the American aircraft, which, had ten portable seats. My seat was taken by another person while I was visiting the toilet because it had more leg room, I just took a seat two rows back, which, as it turns out was a good move. When we landed the man in my seat did not move he had been killed by a long blade through the back of the seat. That blade was intended for me."

"When I arrived home I was forced to remain seated and watch my family being violated by six vicious men until I handed over my formulas which, I did but without the safety notes, hence the large house and laboratory exploding. Later I was captured and held hostage on a boat until I was rescued by you and Bernie.

My family and myself are under a constant threat, whenever we go out for a walk we are followed and I can no longer tolerate this situation, in fact, my wife is on the verge of a nervous breakdown."

"Lance, I am trying to get some normality back in our lives, this is the reason for the plan I have explained to you. What do you think?"

"Personally, I think it is a brave and unselfish thing to do in view of the years you have spent experimenting to arrive at this point."

"The oil producing countries have nothing to fear, the progress that is being made in this field today will open a vast market for their goods."

*

"I understand that Bernie is trying to locate the Speirs brothers, is that so?"

"Yes his peers are still pressing him that they should be captured and punished in the same way as their families were."

"The average German did not agree with what they did, they were vile vicious criminals."

"I was in charge of constructing a launching pad for the flying bombs on a long flat railway wagon the English called them "Doodle Bugs." The idea was that we could move it around to prevent the R.A.F from pinpointing and bombing the launching pad."

"While working on the wagon I saw several railway cattle wagons arrive at the station full of Jewish families, they were dragged out of the wagons on to the platform, lined up before being marched off to the local camp. On arrival they would be made to strip and enter the delousing showers, which, as you know it was a gas chamber. They would get the girls and younger women together and watch as they stripped naked. One of the young women refused to strip in front of Rudd and his group, he pulled out his revolver and shot her dead, no one else refused to obey. Animals would have received better treatment than they did, it was a wicked time."

"Tell Bernie to give me a call in a couple of days and I will have the information he needs. Both Rudd and Bruno will be at the address I will give him. Will he be able to arrest them, has he the authority over any German citizen, he being an Israeli Jew but he could enlist help?"

"Hold on there, don't let us get into the anti Semitic stream again."

"Sorry, I didn't mean it to sound as it came out."

They stopped talking and Lance sat looking at the door but seeing nothing, his mind drifted back to the time he was in hiding in the loft of a village cottage. In his minds eye he could picture Anna's beautiful face and figure when she visited him every evening with his food and they would spend time sat talking. He suddenly realized he missed her and they had become very close, too close under the circumstances. One day, yes one day he would revisit the village and renew his friendship with Anna and the people who were so kind to him while he was hiding in the loft.

Bernie contacted Klaus, asking if Lance had got it right that "He would help him find Rudd and Bruno?"

"Yes Bernie, I have made enquiries and I should have the address you want tomorrow, ring me during the afternoon."

Chapter 24

Bernie telephoned Klaus the following day and Klaus gave him all the information he needed, the address and the evening Rudd and Bruno would be at that address.

Bernie called six of his team to a meeting to arrange a plan of how to carry out an arrest.

Rook telephoned Lance telling him that Rudd had been tipped off about the plan to arrest him and his brother and his supporters were arranging a reception committee. Lance discovered later that Rook had advised both sides of the proposed arrest and collected fees from both sides. Lance had earlier been a little suspicious about Rooks actions and he was sure Rook was playing one side against the other, in the past Rook had passed information a day after the event had taken place causing chaos in the various plans.

*

Bernie had expected his plans to be leaked as too many people knew of his intention to capture the Speirs brothers. He thought he had taken the necessary steps should his team run into difficulties but no one realized what a cat and mouse situation it would become. Lance told Bernie that he could not be relied upon to take part in the operation but he would forward any information that came to light.

Thursday night, Bernie and his team started off to the address given to them. They were travelling down a very quiet road heading for the house. Suddenly they could see two cars side by side with armed men each side blocking off the approach to the house, it was obvious that they had been tipped off about the visit and they were supporters of the brothers. Bernie realized he could not expect his men to try and pass the blockade as they were not armed but suddenly one of the cars exploded into a ball of fire and as that car was dying down the second car exploded and they were two balls of fire. They waited at a distance until the fires had died down a little and they approached but could do nothing for the armed men as the explosion had killed them all. They pushed the wreckage to one side and carried on to the house.

They entered the house but at first they couldn't find anyone but searching around they found the two brothers and several of their supporters cowering in a cupboard under the stairs. They tied the hands of the brothers and just pushed the supporters away while Bernie's men put them in the car.

As they were leaving the house several men approached from across the lawn, one man said "Are you Bernie Black?"

"Yes, why do you ask?"

"My name is Thai and I knew the Speirs had been tipped off and I stepped in and cleared the debt I owed Lance. Kindly tell him."

"Did you explode the cars?"

"Yes, Cheers," and off he went.

The brothers were placed in a car and set off heading for a disused labour camp, on arrival they found the chains had been cut by Bernie's team and the gates were wide open. They motored to the outskirts of the camp until they reached the so called shower units and the cars were brought to a halt. The two brothers were dragged out of the car and taken to the unit and told to strip. Rudd dropped to his knees and started to whine and pleading for his life, Bruno was crying and wailing asking for forgiveness. Bernie almost gave way seeing a human being so terrified but his team pushed them into the chamber and slammed the heavy metal door. Never, when Rudd was designing these chambers did he realize how terrifying they were, with the door closed.

One of his team slid the window shutter open and threw in a gas canister and closed the shutter to. They could hear screaming and shouting but by the time they got into their cars the screaming and shouting had stopped. They then drove off. Bernie was pleased to have carried out his peers' instructions but he felt sickened with whole business.

Chapter 25

Lance was beginning to feel a little home sick and his thoughts kept drifting back to the loft in the village cottage where Anna helped him to remain sane while hiding in the loft after he had been rescued from his burning plane and she helped by scrounging food to take to him each evening. He often wondered if the people who helped him escaped the cruelty of the Germans as they were forced to retreat from France. He decided to contact his senior officer in London to let him leave Berlin after a two year stint and take some leave. He was given permission to take leave but to contact London if he should see any disruption in any of the liberated countries.

Lance visited Max and told him of his decision, Max was disappointed as he had become to look upon Lance as a real friend. Max obtained permission to allow Lance to take a Jeep from the car pool but he must hand it into the American depot in France making sure he obtains a signed receipt when he returns the Jeep to the depot.

Lance would be very disturbed if he knew that Anna was in hiding from a group of three women and two men who had taken it upon themselves to punish any woman who collaborated with the enemy by shaving their heads. Anna had been accused of fraternizing with the enemy and her three year old son was fathered by a German. They did not or would not listen to the explanation of how the child was fathered by a British wartime pilot who had been in hiding from the Germans when his plane had been shot down returning from a bombing raid.

Anna kept hoping against hope that Lance would return as he had promised and help her to start living a normal life again. Lance explained to Ivan of his plans and Ivan could see Lance had thought it all through and he would not be able to convince him to change his mind. Ivan told Lance how much money they had in the kitty but Lance refused to take any money from Ivan. Ivan filled the petrol tank of the Jeep and put several 5gallon jerry cans full of petrol in the back of the Jeep.

*

After motoring for two days Lance arrived in the French village and he made his way to the farm. He walked up to the heavy wooden door and knocked and to his surprise a young lady opened the door. "Hello, can I help you?" a voice from down the corridor "Who is it?" An elderly man walked up to the door, he saw Lance he stepped forward and gave Lance a hug.

He pointed to the Jeep "Is that yours?"

"Yes"

"Right, take me to the market place, Anna and nineteen women are being held there by a group, they say that they are carrying out vengeance on the females who collaborated with the Germans by shaving their heads. We must hurry."

They arrived at the market place and there were twenty women sat on ten chairs back to back. The farmer pointed out Anna to Lance, he immediately went forward to Anna embraced and kissed her she was overcome and started crying. One of the women wielding a large pair of scissors tried to push Lance away but he refused to budge.

Lance shouted in a very loud voice, "How, can you accuse this lady of liasing with the Germans. My name is Flying Officer Franks of the British R.A.F. When I crashed here returning to the UK from a bombing raid, this lady pulled me from a burning plane and took me to the farm, she tended to my burns and the local doctor set my broken shoulder and then she hid me in the loft of a cottage and nursed me back to health. She had great difficulty in finding enough food to feed me each night. The little boy is my son." Lance pulled Anna to her feet and marched away from the chairs, no one tried to stop them. When he looked down at the small boy, he was shocked he thought he was looking into a mirror. The farmer put his arm around Anna and they all piled into the Jeep and drove back to the farm.

As they approached the farm they could see Josie, the farmer's wife looking for them through the window. As Lance got out of the Jeep Josie came dashing out of the house and hugged Lance. "I am so pleased you have returned as you promised you would. We have never forgotten you we just looked at Lance Junior." When they got inside the house, Albert the farmer nodded to Lance to follow him, they entered the small barn along the side of the farm, Albert moved several bales of straw exposing a small door. The farmer unlocked the small door and entered the room. There were several meat carcasses, legs of pork and hams hanging from metal rails. He took down a leg of pork and handed it to Anna who had followed them into the barn. Albert pulled down a large tarpaulin and Lance could see several small barrels and racks of wine bottles. Albert squeezed round the back of the bottles and pulled out a bottle of cognac and promptly produced two glasses and filled them. Lance claimed he had never tasted a better cognac. "How on earth did you manage to keep all this wine safe from the Nazi troops, they usually plundered any food store or wine cellars?"

"Lance would you have found the small door? We kept you safe in the loft and I kept my wines safe in the basemen?" Smiling as he said it.

*

We have a problem Lance, he went over to the corner of the barn and removed a pile of hay and he saw the dead body of a Nazi Officer. There are several farms involved in his death but I got left with his body. Lance smiled, "Have you still got the furnace in the basement?"

"Yes"

"Burn all his clothes except his tunic. Ask Pierre to put twenty of his pigs in one pen and delay their feed this evening. Will he do this without question Albert?"

"Yes we understand each other."

"Strip him and burn his clothes and we will take his body and his tunic to Pierre's tonight, make sure the tunic is badly torn making it look as if the pigs have eaten part of it."

"I will send a message to Pierre straight away"

As the darkness closed in they put the body in the Jeep and took it to Hill Top Farm, Pierre indicated which pen to use. They tipped the body into the pen and

the squealing and grunting was earsplitting as they pounced on the body to attack it. Albert turned to Lance, "There will be nothing left by the morning, if any bones are left Pierre will put them in his grinder and spread the bone meal on his fields."

"As a matter of interest Albert how did the officer die?"

Looking at Lance, Albert hesitated.

"As you might know there are still groups of SS Storm Troopers roaming around and this officer was with one of these groups. The farmer's wife was in the barn feeding the chickens when this officer entered the barn and attempted to rape her. She was screaming and trying to push him away, her 10year old son came dashing in, he jumped on the officers back but the officer swung his arm backwards hitting the boy in the face and knocking him to the floor dazed. As the boy went to get up his hand fell on a pitch fork handle, he jumped up and drove the sharp prongs into the back of the officer, he had used so much force that the points of the prongs were protruding from his chest at the front. All the farmers closed ranks. That is how it happened, Lance."

They went into the kitchen where Josie had the meal ready and on the table were glasses and several bottles of wine. "This is a celebration meal for your return Lance."

Chapter 26

"Albert, may I speak to you and Josie privately?"

"Certainly Lance." They went into an adjoining room.

"I am going to be quite honest with you both. I would like your permission to marry your daughter Anna but at the present time I have no money and my future prospects are uncertain. I have a university degree in languages and I will be entitled to a substantial back pay from the time I spent in hiding and working for the secret service in Berlin, they employed me prior to joining the RAF. I have no parents, they were both killed in a car crash when I was small and I was brought up by an Aunt and Uncle. I have told you exactly my circumstances hoping you will allow me to marry Anna?"

"Lance, we are both more than happy to embrace you into our family, we feel sure that you will make a good husband and father and you will look after our daughter. The question of cash, don't you worry, I will help you until you get back on your feet again."

"Do you plan to get married in this village, or are you thinking of going home first?"

"The choice is entirely Anna's, I rather think she will choose this village, I have told you I have no family to invite, that is apart from my Aunt and Uncle, if they are still living. I don't know what to expect when I go home."

*

Lance telephoned Max asking if he could get permission for him to keep the Jeep for a few more days and hand it back in a car pool in England. He is going and to look up his only relative who took care of him when his parents were killed. Max came straight back and told Lance to hand the Jeep into the car pool in Ruislip, which, is on the outskirts of London when he has completed his search. Lance was delighted with this arrangement.

Lance and Anna discussed their plans for the wedding and they decided to hold it in the village, it has been a year or so since the village had any excitement. When the villagers heard about the wedding they all started making plans to make it a real celebration with the Wedding Breakfast and entertainment. Albert joked with Josie saying his stocks of wine and food would take a beating. The local priest was delighted to be asked to make the necessary arrangements for the wedding to take place in his church. The next problem Anna came up against was a suitable wedding garment but here again the villagers suddenly produced suitable material, in fact, the village started to buzz and excitement began to build. On the day of the wedding, it was warm and sunny and the village square was decked out with coloured bunting and long tables, obviously no one had been invited, the villagers invited themselves. After the church wedding the food and wine was available in abundance, the musicians played their heart out for all the dancing, eating and drinking until the early hours of the morning, eventually the villagers started making their way home, some walking straight and a large number staggering.

*

The morning after the wedding they had an early breakfast hoping to make an early start, Lance brought the Jeep round to the front of house and he was pleasantly surprised, the petrol tank had been filled and the two five gallon jerry cans had also been refilled, by whom or from where, no one admitted knowing. They put what little luggage they had into the Jeep and Anna and Marco joined Lance but they got out again to say their good bys. Lance promised to be back in a few days time. They had no difficulty in getting a place on a ship heading for Dover, the Americans were moving a lot of equipment back to England before shipping it back to the States. To avoid any confusion they kept referring to Lance junior as Marco and that was how he was introduced to the authorities when they arrived in Dover.

They decided to book into a hotel just outside Dover for the night, each time Lance spent any money he made a note so as to repay Albert on his return. They had a good evenings rest and they were up early and ready to depart towards Guildford. Lance recognized the area where his Auntie lives and the house in which he was brought up. He was still a little uncertain what to expect, he left the Jeep two streets away they walked down the street and up the drive to the front door of the house.

Lance rang the door bell and moved around the corner of the building leaving Marco on the doorstep.

An elderly frail looking lady opened the door keeping her hand on the door post for support and she looked down.

"Good God, my little Lance", as she bent forward to hug him she started to fall, Lance stepped forward and caught her to prevent her falling. She looked at Lance, tears started to well in her eyes and looking into his eyes a big smile crossed her face and she hugged him. "Lance, I have waited years for this moment, we never knew what had happened to you. Do come in." When they got inside the house he introduced Anna and Marco to his Auntie Hilda and she cuddled Marco and refused to let him go, it was obvious she would spoil Marco rotten.

They went inside the house and Hilda was so excited to have Lance home, she thought he had been killed like so many of her friend's families. Ted had been killed during a daylight raid when his workplace received a direct hit killing all the workers. They sat talking for hours and Lance told Hilda how Anna had pulled him from a burning plane and hidden him from the Germans. Hilda and Marco could not speak the same language but somehow appeared to understand each other. Hilda insisted that they should stay with her while Lance attempts to sort his work situation out. Lance was uncertain where to go and he had very little money so he was delighted with the offer. It was decided that Anna and Marco should stay with Hilda while Lance went to London and reported to Colonel Snaith's office. Anna was very happy with the situation as she felt so at ease in Hilda's company and she could take a lot of weight off Hilda's shoulders by cooking and cleaning, which, Hilda had neglected due to her restricted mobility.

Lance telephoned Whitehall to make an appointment with Colonel Snaith, he was really hoping to all his back pay and an offer of a new position.

Chapter 27

Lance travelled to London leaving Anna and Marco with Hilda he was completely relaxed with the situation. Hilda and Anna appeared to be happy in each others company. Arriving at Whitehall he was shown into the main reception area and waited to be called. Ten minutes later a young lady called his name and invited him to follow, he followed her up a long stairway, along a dark corridor and was shown into a large expensive looking office and told to sit in a comfortable armchair and wait. Colonel Snaith entered the office he walked up to Lance raising his hand to shake hands. "Lance, we have spoken many times on the phone but this is the first time we have met face to face, come with me."

They walked together into a small side office and an American Army officer was sitting at a desk, he was introduced as Major Bruce.

"We are delighted you have arrived we need a linguist to deal with a job in Paris. There are organized gangs carrying out a protection racket with the businesses as they are just setting up again. To make matters worse there are two gangs and we feel the competition will escalate into a violent situation and we do not want violence to erupt on the streets of Paris, we have enough trouble to contend with without gang warfare."

Colonel turned to Lance "I am given to understand that you have recently got married to a French girl."

"Yes, my wife pulled me out my burning plane when I crashed returning from a bombing raid over Germany and her parents hid me in the loft of their farm until the war ended. This young lady scrounged food to feed me each night, we became very close and we have a small son, Marco.

"I would like you to live in Paris, accommodation can be arranged, Major Bruce will arrange for your Jeep to be collected and replaced with a new one together with the necessary documents to obtain petrol. Are you prepared to take this position?"

"I would be pleased to undertake the offer do you have any other agents working on this problem In Paris? When would you want me to start?"

"One thing I failed to mention is that you will wear your R.A.F. Officers uniform, with a shoulder flash indicating you belong to the intelligence corp. All I can tell you at the moment is that the gang leaders are either German or Polish, at one stage we thought the Russians were involved but according to the information received they are not. We must stamp this nonsense out before it becomes nasty. We have had enough trouble on the streets."

"I realize we are still close allies with America Forces but why is Major Bruce involved with my being sent to Paris?" The Major stood up.

"I can understand your question Lance but I am here to tell you that two American Officers that you have had dealings with in the past are involved in the protection racket in Paris." Lance stood up and wiped his brow.

"Good God, have they escaped from prison?"

"No they didn't escape, the President was persuaded to overrule the courts decision and they have been released and what is more they are in Paris. The President decided on the old adage "Set a thief to catch a thief". I appreciate your dealings with our two officers was not a happy one but you will have to put your differences behind you."

"I will try Sir but knowing your two officers are both dishonest and no doubt they will soon be in charge of the protection gangs working for their own good, we shall see in time." The Major just glared at Lance.

"You speak very disrespectful of two of the American Army Officers selected by our President to investigate."

"Major they are both dishonest crooks."

*

Major Bruce and Colonel Snaith walked down to the basement car park with Lance and the Major pointed out a brand new Jeep to Lance and handed him the keys. "You will find that this Jeep is more powerful than the one you have been driving."

" I want you to stay overnight while the outfitters sort you out with your new officer's kit." Lance was taken to the outfitter and he was given the uniform and whatever an officer of his rank is entitled to. The following morning he enjoyed a first class breakfast in the officer's mess. He was told that he was to report to Colonel Snaith before he left the offices. When he reported, the Colonel wished him well and sent him off to the treasury department. A young lady there had all his papers ready for him to approve the back pay due to him. As he got out of his seat, the young lady gave him a large sum of money in French Francs. She looked at him smiling "This should tide you over until you next visit a Pay Masters office." He thought that he must have looked peculiar with the look of surprise on his face. Lance got into his Jeep and headed for Guildford, he was looking forward to seeing Anna and Marco again. Anna was very surprised to see Lance arrive wearing a brand new uniform and a new Jeep. Her eyes quizzed him but he said "I will tell you the full story when we get underway."

*

It was a very tearful departure when they left Hilda's house. She had got so used to Lance and his family being with her although it had only been for few days. Anna invited Hilda to go with them and she assured Hilda that she would be made most welcome to stay at the farm for a while. Hilda smiled, "Thank you but I don't feel well enough to travel, another time perhaps." Anna was reluctant to leave her but she had to go. When they arrived back in Dover Lance had no difficulty in securing passage for his family and his Jeep when he showed the necessary paper work.

Arriving back at the farm the farmer and his wife were delighted to see their daughter and her family again but they were surprised to see Lance in uniform. Lance was a little uncertain whether or not to take Anna and Marco to Paris with him. He felt he would be happier if he should go to the flat that had been prepared for his arrival also he wanted to ensure the streets were safe for Anna and Marco to live in Paris with him. Anna and Lance discussed it and they decided that Lance should go alone at first and Anna and Marco will join him later if he considered it to be safe.

Chapter 28

The morning Lance was leaving for Paris they both had certain misgivings at the prospect of being apart for a while. However when Lance arrived in Paris he was pleasantly surprised where the flat was situated, together with his own secure parking place. When he entered the flat itself he was again surprised, it had been decorated and equipped with all the latest kitchen appliances and the windows at the back looking out over countryside not buildings. He smiled when he saw the large amount of wardrobe space for Anna to fill in the main bedroom. He checked the telephone and was pleased to find it was connected, he rang a number he had been given to meet up with an agent who would bring him up to speed. When he spoke to the man they arranged to go for a drink to meet, just two blocks from the flat.

Lance called upon his training as an agent he put a small caliber revolver in his pocket, just as insurance. He walked past the café twice weighing up the area, he felt reasonably safe with the situation so he entered the café bar. He found a small table, he sat with his back against a wall facing the main door to view who walks in, these things he did automatically as they were drummed into him while training, watch your back! The waiter had just put his coffee and brandy down on his table when he thought he recognized a man who walked into the bar. However, the man walked up to Lance's table. "May I join you?"

"Certainly, pull up a chair." The man ordered his drink and turned to Lance. "Where have we met before?" Lance was being wary, he thought he had met this man before but was it as a friend or foe?

"I can't say but I was a prisoner of war and now I'm working here to make sure our men are safe and helped to return home." Lance thought to himself, where did I get that tale from? It does sound feasible, I hope he thinks so, He! He! The man looked at Lance and smiled, "Bernie told me you were cagey. We met at a meeting trying to decide who was responsible for goods going astray when they landed in Berlin. The two people present who were regarded as suspicious were Brigadier Bolton and Colonel Bradbury and oddly enough they have become the main players in the protection game here that someone is playing. We thought they were supposed to be getting to the bottom of the problem but they are now running the organization and they are bullet proof, the President of America sent them on a special assignment to put a stop to the protection racket. Before we go any further, let me introduce myself, my name is Simon and I am a member of Bernie Blacks team, or should I say, one of his worldly tentacles and he has given me this letter of introduction," handing Lance an envelope. Lance read the letter and he immediately felt comfortable working with Simon. Bernie had included his clever identity scribble, which Lance recognized.

*

Brigadier Bolton had surrounded himself with a team of thugs and his men arrested the man who they thought was the main gang leader, I should say kidnapped him and he was taken to an old disused hospital. The Brigadier and Brad instructed that the man should be sat on a chair and his hands would be tied at the back of the chair and each leg tied to a chair leg. They dismissed their men leaving the two of them to deal with the gang leader.

Looking straight at the man in the chair, Brad said "What is your name?"

"My name is Hal, why do you need to know?" He replied.

"We want the list of business's you get money from and the dates you call on them." Hal looked at them and just laughed, "So would many other people like that list, "Go! to hell?" Brad punched Hal hard in his face, breaking his nose and it started pouring with blood. They punched and kicked Hal but he would not give in, his face looked a terrible mess.

The door opened and a man walked in pushing a wheelchair and the lady sat in the chair started screaming when she saw his bloody face. Hal looked up, "Don't you cry they won't get want they want from me."

Hal said, "Leave my wife out of this, she has no idea about my work. You can't involve my wife as she has Osteoporosis which has made her have thin brittle bones and she is ill."

The Brigadier just smiled, he leaned forward offering his hands to her, when she put her hands in his thinking it was a kind gesture he jerked her to her feet, as this happened they all heard a loud crack, he had broken her left arm and she looked so distressed and the broken bone was protruding the flesh.

Hal shouted! "Stop, leave my wife alone. You get an ambulance here to take my wife to the hospital and I will give you the combination number to my safe, you will find all you need there."

They called an ambulance and when his wife was on the way to the hospital he wrote the combination number down and handed it to Brad.

*

The two officers went off laughing and jumped into their Jeep and set off to Hal's address. They entered the house and after looking around they found the safe in the cellar. They stood looking at each other laughing and rubbing their hands. They fed the numbers into the lock and again leaning towards the safe they smiled and their faces were close, ready to look inside the safe. Brad opened the safe door, as it opened there was a small explosion and their faces were sprayed with acid. They were both screaming and stumbling around as the acid had blinded them. They stumbled outside on to the road and a passer by called the police and an ambulance and they were taken off to hospital screaming in pain.

The Brigadier's team called at the old disused hospital the following evening and they were very surprised to find Hal still tied in the chair with his nose still trickling blood. His face was in a shocking state with all the cuts and bruising. They untied him, gave him a drink of water and some chocolate that is all they had with them. Hal had great difficulty walking so between them they half carried and walked Hal out on to the street and sat him on a seat in a bus shelter. They called the police saying he had been attacked by a group of youths and requires medical attention.

Hal was taken to a hospital where they stitched his gashes and cauterized his bleeding nose and it was decided to give him a blood infusion.

When Hal started feeling better he kept asking about his wife, when he finally got an answer he insisted that he should be allowed to visit her. His wife was delighted when she saw him walk into the ward. She looked at him with her head tilted to one side. "Did you give in?" he smiled, "Well yes and no, I gave them the combination number of a safe which will have punished them." She smiled but said no more.

Lance received a message from Simon saying that he had heard one of the gang leaders named Hal had been admitted to hospital after being roughed up. Lance decided to investigate. He went to the hospital and was shown into the ward where Hal was lying in a bed. As he approached his bed Lance was appalled by the state of Hal's face, "Good lord who did this to you?"

"The two American Army Officers who wanted all my paper work relating to the businesses I protect from the protection gangs. They wanted the dates we call to collect their insurance payments." Lance started laughing. "Hal who is protecting whom, this is a comical situation they are paying protection twice hoping to survive." Hal looked up at Lance. "As you can see they beat me, when I refused to give them the details, they brought my wife into the room and started on her by breaking her arm. I gave them what they wanted, the combination numbers to my safe in the cellar at my home address but it didn't contain what they wanted."

*

"This safe was one of twenty placed around Paris which had a booby trap. The booby trap that was inserted was known to only one member of the French Resistance Group, he had installed the safes, bolted to the wall about 5feet eight inches from the floor hoping to create the maximum impact to the intruder. The safe doors had a thin white line across it and the locals knew this and would not touch any safe showing the thin line.

The reason for this precaution was because a very senior Nazi Officer had been entering houses torturing to get the safe details then shooting the occupants and emptying the safe. I gave them the number of that safe hoping it would explode and kill them, did it kill them?"

"No it didn't kill them, when they opened the safe there was a four second delay then an explosion activated a small pump and the intruders were sprayed with acid."

"So it didn't kill them?"

"No, but it has badly disfigured their faces, they are now both blind." Hal started to laugh, "That is better still."

*

Lance left the hospital and when he arrived back at his flat he telephoned Colonel Snaith they both enjoyed a laugh when Lance explained how Hal's team are in fact protecting the business from the protection gangs demanding money. No money, the business premises would be damaged or set on fire.

Lance then told the Colonel how the two American officers had tortured Hal until they got the combination of his safe. "They went to his house and opened the safe, there was a four second delay and an explosion activated a small pump spraying acid in their faces. They are both badly disfigured and they have lost their eyesight."

"That is sad Lance."

"Yes I would agree with you but what is the world coming to, we had a war to get some sort of order in our lives but is the phoney war ever going to end?"

"I understand the Parisian police are getting to grips with gang warfare and the organizers, or should I say gang leaders. Several of these men have been arrested and being kept in prison indefinitely while their activities are being investigated. One such man has been in prison 3 months so far."

*

"I would like to talk to you about a job that has cropped up and you might be interested in. The job will entail you working as my right hand man and as an interpreter sitting in on the many meetings being planned. It would mean you relocating to London but the accommodation will be good and an excellent school place will be made available for Marco. One very good point is the streets of London are safe for you and your family. If you preferred you could commute from Guildford if you would rather."

"I am very interested in your offer but before I give you my answer, let me discuss it with Anna. She would find it very different living in a city after living on a farm in the French countryside."

Chapter 29

Lance telephoned Anna promising to return home in two days and he intends staying at home for ten days leave. Colonel Snaith has offered me a position as his deputy it will involve acting as an interpreter at many meetings planned in the near future. The position will involve relocation to London. I have not accepted the offer yet I told him that I wanted to discuss the upset of moving with you first. Give it some thought and then when I get home we can talk it over. We could stay with Hilda in Guildford and I could commute by train to London. One of the sweeteners' offered is that a place will be made available for Marco in an excellent school. I have not made a decision yet we will discus it when I get home. I promise I will do nothing to upset our happy family life. He placed the phone back on its cradle and sat back in his chair, lost in thought.

*

The phone started ringing interrupting his reverie, picking up the phone a man's voice said "Am I talking to Lance Goodchild?"

"Yes and who are you?"

"This is Max."

"Good Lord, I didn't recognize your voice. It is great to hear from you. How are you, hope you are keeping well?"

"Yes I am well but I have some disturbing news for you. Klaus has come up with a Ground to Air missile, it is much smaller but when tested it is just as effective, in fact it is devastating. The launching system will fit into the boot of a family car making it a mobile destructive weapon and the missile itself is the size of a Jaffa orange and he is now working on it to make it Heat Seeking. Having told you this everyone is on the jump as a Korean consortium has offered a large sum of money for the "KNOW HOW," to enable them to manufacture without paying Royalties. "JOKE" Can you imagine them obeying any man made laws? So once again we are in a dangerous situation, Klaus has only recently overcome the threat to his person because of the Rocket fuel. Klaus is a family name,

Klaus Gunter died in a nursing home eighteen months ago this must be Klaus Bordman his cousin. They are all scientists."

"Yes Max it could be nasty. Incidentally, did Major Bruce contact you regarding the Jeep? They have issued me with a new more powerful one."

"Yes Lance it was all sorted, all the paper work was dealt with, transferring the Jeep to a London Depot."

*

Anna was faced with a dilemma, should she go to London with her husband Lance, or should she remain loyal to her parents and stay at the farm and care for them as they are now getting older.

She sat thinking back to the time she realized that she was pregnant and Lance was no longer in the loft, there were no recrimination from her parents. They were supportive throughout her pregnancy and during the birth of Marco. The first year of his life was a very difficult one, the Allies were pushing the German Army out of France their supply route was cut off and marauding groups of soldiers entered houses and farms stealing food or wine or whatever they could find to eat to stay alive.

The villagers were alerted of an approaching group of soldiers the ladies from neighbouring farms came to Albert's farm and hid in the converted loft until they had left. Albert decided to sacrifice some of his foodstuff and wines he put two small barrels of wine, a ham, three loaves of bread, cheese and butter in the corner of the small barn. It gave the impression of being a hidden food store but the soldiers will easily find it and they will think it is the farmer's secret store.

The women arrived and they went to the loft, Anna and her mother went into the loft with them. They had just got settled when the soldiers came charging in ransacking the cupboards, suddenly a cheer went up, they had found the store room. They ripped the top off one of the barrels and started eating and drinking like a pack of wild animals. In fact, it was like a party, shouting and singing and the drunken leader of the group held a gun to Albert's head asking, "Where are all the women?"

"They are all in the market place." The leader shouted, "Come along, we will go to the market place. I want the tank and the people carriers driven across the vineyard", as they were crashing through the vines, Albert stood with tears in his eye's they were destroying years of work.

The soldiers were disappointed when they arrived at the market place, there were no womenfolk to be seen they were just about to leave when they saw a young lady hanging washing out on a line. They pounced on her and started to brutally rape the young girl. There were fifteen ladies hiding in a flat overlooking the square, when they saw what was happening one of the ladies said "Come on, enough is enough." They grabbed wooden chair and table legs from broken furniture and dashed down into the square and they started beating the soldiers, they had no chance against the ladies fury and the fact the soldiers were drunk. In no time at all the soldiers looked a bloody mess and the ladies beat them one by one in their most vulnerable part of their anatomy, this should put them off the urge for sex for a while and in some cases for ever. The soldiers retreated quickly but most were crawling as they were unable to walk and many of these tough guys were crying for mercy. Anna smiled to herself when she recalled the story as the ladies told the tale.

Chapter 30

Anna was surprised and delighted when she saw a jeep pull up outside the main gate of the farm and Lance got out. Marco dashed out to greet him and Anna was standing by the door, she threw her arms around his neck expressing her pleasure at his returning home. "I am home for ten days holiday that is unless your father needs any help." Josie and Albert entered the room to greet him he was now accepted as a member of the family.

When they sat alone Lance turned to Anna. "Have you made a decision, do we stay here or are we going to London to live?" smiling as he said it.

"Lance I keep turning the move over in my mind, I just don't know. What are your feelings?"

"It will be a big upheaval for you to moving into a city when you are used to living in the countryside. I am home for ten days shall we forget it for the moment and enjoy each other and Marco?"

Josie went into the kitchen where Anna was by herself, she put her arm around her. "Have you made a decision about London yet?"

"No nothing definite as yet."

"Anna I realize it will be a wrench to leave here but you should be at the side of your husband. We will miss you terribly but you must put you own family first now."

*

Lance had two days left of his leave so they sat down and discussed the move and decided to move to London for a six month trial. If Anna fails to settle, Lance has promised to leave the job and they will return to France.

Lance contacted Hilda asking if they could stay with her for the six month trial. She replied by return saying how delighted she would be to have them stay with her, no doubt Hilda would be pleased to have company.

When Anna told Josie and Albert of her decision, they were both disappointed but the realized that she had her own life and family to consider. Lance promised they would make frequent visits to ensure they were both well and able to continue working the farm. Lance was well aware that he had a lot to thank them for they had hid him in the loft. If he had been discovered they would have been shot and goodness knows what would have happened to Anna.

Lance contacted Colonel Snaith to tell him he would like to accept his offer of a new position and that he would be staying with his Aunt in Guildford and commuting.

Right Lance I will arrange with the education people about an opening for Marco but the final decision of which school, will be yours. There are several good schools in that area, in fact, I am given to understand you attended one of the schools when you lost your family.

*

Lance joined the Colonel's office in Paris and he was sat in the restaurant next door when a man came up to his table, "May I join you?"

"Certainly, I would be glad of your company, I have yet to meet the people working in these offices."

"A friend of mine who lives in Marlow, asked me to check you out when I told him I was joining this office."

"That is odd why would anybody be interested in me?"

"My name is Ken and you are Lance, is that correct?"

"Yes."

Ken then told him the full story of how Frank Haines found three R.A.F. Tunics in the loft of a farm cottage he had bought and was renovating. Two of the owners were found and were delighted to have the tunics returned but he was unable to trace the third one. The name on the tab inside the tunic was Flying Officer Goodchild which, would have belonged to you.

"I wonder what happened to the tunic?"

"Ken I am most grateful you have told me this story. I will try and visit Frank in Marlow when I find his address, I might even meet him when he visits the farm cottage. I wonder if he still has the tunic?"

"I can tell you he hasn't, the Air Ministry sent a man to Frank's address with an authorizing letter to commandeer the tunic and he took it away draped over his arm."

"I am really intrigued, I must look into this, the plot thickens" said Lance laughing.

*

Lance went back into his office only to find a message from Colonel Snaith to phone him. When Lance did manage to speak to the Colonel he was surprised when he was told the meetings he was to attend were to be held at the Palace de Versailles in ten days time and he was advised to book a room in a local hotel in readiness. The Colonel said "The European countries are all sending an Ambassador, with all the different tongues you will be kept on your toes." Lance heard him laughing as he put the phone down.

Lance decided to go back to the farm and bring Anna and Marco to the flat in Paris. They could spend some time together before the meetings start and Anna could be introduced to the flat.

Josie persuaded Anna to leave Marco with her at the farm, to which both Anna and Lance agreed so as not to disrupt his schooling.

Anna and Lance left the farm and headed towards Paris, Lance was looking forward to introducing Anna to the flat. When they arrived at the flat Anna was delighted how so well organized it was with all the up to date appliances. Lance pulled her leg as he showed her all the wardrobe space for her to fill.

Several days later they decided to go to the hotel next to the venue where the meetings were to take place. When they booked in at the desk Anna was overcome by the opulence after the austere conditions they had become accustomed to during the war and the enemy occupation. Lance accused Anna of going back to her childhood as she jumped on the bed because it was so comfortable and the way she ran around in the expensive looking bathroom. Naturally Lance was delighted and relieved to find Anna at ease and excited with the change of living scenery.

The first meeting was more of an exploratory exercise to find what they all wanted to discuss. Lance realized why the Colonel laughed as he put the phone down, the languages certainly posed Lance with a problem. It wasn't the languages that bothered Lance but the different dialects the ambassadors used.

When the meeting came to a close, they all went into another room where the wives were enjoying a buffet and drinks. It is always difficult to have conversation with a colleague in a crowded room but in this case it was the many languages being spoken at the same time. Every time Anna looked up a man was looking at her and this went on and it made Anna very uncomfortable, quietly she told Lance how uncomfortable this man was making her feel. Lance rose from his chair and went across to the man. "My name is Lance Goodchild and you are?"

"My name is Karl Steiner, why do you ask?"

"You are making my wife very uncomfortable with you constantly staring at her, do you know her?" Looking at Lance "Don't you realize what my looks to your wife conveys?"

"No I don't"

"Retreating German soldiers and the Russian army troops are guilty of raping and treating the French women in a disgusting manner. A group of these ladies got together and they blew up a part of the barracks killing the soldiers responsible for the disgusting treatment issued to three of these women. They do not wear a uniform but they all wear Blue jeans, Check Shirt, Blue Neckerchief and they wear Shades."

"What the hell are shades?"

"Don't you know?"

"No what are they?"

"Sun Glasses,"

"Good Lord, I am behind the times."

"What you are saying, my wife has unknowingly dressed in the same manner as these ladies. I must point this error out to her but her dress has nothing to do with the ladies Revenge Group." Laughing, Karl said "I won't keep looking at your beautiful wife because of her dress, it's because she is so attractive."

"I am pleased to hear you say that, I must watch you myself if you admire my wife so much."

"Yes you should, she is such a wonderful woman and I know you would be very sad to lose her."

"Are you saying that I don't look after her?"

"I and a team will be visiting a farm near your in-laws the Allies insist that we remove all the ammunition and explosive material from a barn on one of the farms where it had been stored."

"Just you keep your eye on your wife."

"Are you making threats against my wife?"

"No, just be careful, take good care of her and be very careful not to upset a powerful person." He then walked away. Lance found this conversation very disturbing even a little threatening, he must check on Karl Steiner.

When Anna and Lance arrived back to their hotel room, Lance explained to her about her dress attracting the man's attention to look at her. "He told me not to upset a powerful person otherwise it would have repercussions on your health."

"Good heavens Lance, is that a threat?"

"I know that man from somewhere in the past, I have been racking my brain but I can't remember where or when."

They had both found it to be a trying day so they decided on an early night. In the early hours of the morning Anna woke with a start and she saw Karl Steiner standing at the bottom of her bed wearing a Gestapo uniform, she blinked and he was gone.

Chapter 31

Waking up with a start, as she did, she just laid in bed unable get settled again. She started thinking of happenings of the past she and four other women had been trained by the Resistance Group to operate a radio link between them and London. They were trained how to maintain and operate a radio transmitting set. The set was powered by a battery and the radio was in one of the ten chicken huts on her families' farm. The electricity supply was unreliable as the Germans were reluctant to use either oil or coal to feed the power stations.

The battery for the radio was kept fully charged by using a mobile generator, which they kept in a child's wheelbarrow. The reason for having such a generator was to keep the batteries fully charged in the incubators to hatch the chicken eggs and make sure new chicks come along to replace the older hens when they stop laying eggs. The Germans had their radio detecting van out one evening and they traced a call when one of the girls was sending a message and they were able to pinpoint the position of the radio. A German people's carrier speeded round to the farm just as the two girls were leaving the group of chicken huts. A group of Gestapo soldiers grabbed the two girls and wanted to know where the radio set was. All the women of the village were rounded up and made to stand in a circle to watch the two women being interrogated. The girls were repeatedly beaten with long rubber truncheons, one of the girls started to weaken and the interrogator increased his beatings but the girl went limp, it was obvious to the other ladies the girl was dead, they started shouting and surged towards the man wielding the truncheon. They escaped on board the people's carrier, just before one of them jumped on the carrier, he hit one of the women's legs, they all heard the crack of her leg bone being broken but unfortunately it was not a clean break and the lady was sentenced to a wheelchair. They all agreed, "One Day" they would pay the animals back for what they have done today and the man who wielded the truncheon would die a cruel and painful death."

Anna heard that Karl Steiner and his crew were coming back to a neighbouring farm to collect the people carriers that had been garaged there and to remove all the explosive materials.

She passed on the information on to the women folk in the village and they had a meeting and decided two girls at a time would keep a look out for him to arrive. Two days later an armoured division arrived and Karl Steiner was the officer in charge of parking the vehicles and where the troops would live and be fed. The ladies watched his activities very carefully for several days and they decided to kidnap him when he staggered out of a Café Bar late one evening, this appeared to be happening most nights.

The fifth night they waited outside the Café Bar for Karl, as he staggered out of a bar five ladies jumped on him. One put a hood over his head, another pulled his hands behind his back and placed an old pair of handcuffs on him and they bundled him into a farm handcart. Having got him helpless they looked at the girl in the wheelchair. "Push him into the forest and I will tell you when to stop." The people pushing the handcart were getting a little perturbed, "How much farther?"

The lady in the wheelchair stopped by a large tree, "Right here, undress him and tie him securely to the tree in a sitting down position."

When they stopped two ladies stepped forward with two cans and several brushes. "Paint him with this oil."

"What is it?"

"Truffle oil. When the wild boars come out to feed on the Truffles it should make an interesting evening for Karl." Karl looked up.

"Please don't do this to me I beg you, please don't do it."

The ladies took no notice of him and carried on pouring the oil over him and around the tree and they could hear the wild animals roaming around in the undergrowth. Karl was screaming to be released. "Come along girls let us get away from these animals." Some of the women were beginning to have second thoughts about the way Karl was being treated, the lady in the wheelchair forcibly made her point by pointing to her legs and the chair. "We have waited eighteen months for the "One Day" we had promised ourselves, today is that day."

*

Several days later Lance and Anna returned to the farm, the village was buzzing with the news of a dead body being found sat down leaning against a tree trunk. The body had been badly mutilated by one or more animals. Anna just smiled, the ladies "One Day" had arrived and he would not be staring at her again.

Lance was still intrigued by what he had been told about his R.A.F Tunic. He strolled across to the row cottages and he saw a man busy in his small garden. "Hello, are you Bob?"

"Yes. How can I help you?"

"I am given to understand that you are friends with Frank Haines?"

"Yes we are friends, he will be in number 2 tomorrow, have you a problem?"

"Not at all, I was told that he found some RAF uniform tunics when he started renovating No2?"

"Sorry I can't help you there as he never did discuss that with me, I must say that it was unusual, he did talk to me about most things."

Two days later Frank walked across to the farm, he knocked on the large heavy wooden door. Anna answered the door. "Can I help you?"

"Yes, is Lance Goodchild living here?"

"I will fetch him, please come in." When Lance entered the room, Frank said

"Are you Flying Officer Goodchild?"

"Yes I am." Frank Smiled

"I am so pleased to meet you my local RAF Association spent a long time trying to trace you to enable me to return your tunic I found in No2. In fact, I found three tunics, two have been returned to the original owners but your tunic was taken from me by the British Secret Service, only you will know why.

That is all water under the bridge now but we will have dinner one evening and I will relate the stories told by the other two." It was arranged before Frank and Beth planned to return home. When a dinner party was mentioned Albert and Josie insisted that the dinner would be held at the farmhouse in view of the room.

The dinner party was a huge success every one was in a happy frame of mind until Lance wanted to hear the stories told by the two airmen who had survived long enough to get their tunics back from Frank. The room fell silent while the two stories were being told, Lance said "Thank you." Two of the ladies were wiping tears from their eyes.

During the meal they enjoyed Albert's wine from his own vinery and he even parted with some of his Brandy. They sat talking and the time was slipping away, Albert stood up saying, "I want you all to join me in drinking a glass of Red Wine from six special vines, I have not tried this wine myself yet. I grafted the cuttings given to me by a friend on six vines just before he was killed. For some reason the Gestapo sprayed his crop and then set fire to his vineyard and his bottling plant. Josie passed him the glasses, when he had poured the wine into all the glasses and passed them round, Albert said "The toast is to my friend Jacque." They all followed suit and drank the wine. Lance looked up, "Albert this is the finest Red Wine I have ever tasted, it is a real world beater." They all agreed with Lance and they all started clapping hands. "I am delighted with your response but unfortunately I only have one small barrel of this wine. I should have grafted more but it is a backbreaking job and my fingers are no longer nimble enough to bind the grafts with raffia to the main stem. Grafting, is as I have said a painstaking job and very few people have the patience. As you are all so supportive with this wine I will try and employ a young person and train him in the grafting skills. Now hostilities are calming down." Lance was so taken with the red wine merchandising plans started ticking over in his head. He thought that he would give it a lot of thought and discuss the plan forming in his head with Albert. What would be the new name given to the red wine?

Chapter 32

When they returned into their room Lance asked Anna to sit down as he wanted to discuss what he had on his mind. She sat down and looked at Lance smiling, "Now what."

"I think that the red wine we enjoyed tonight has a great potential and I think there would be a great market for it. What is your opinion of my helping your father to graft the vine cuttings from the six he has to expand his red wine production. I have no knowledge of farming a vineyard but I feel sure your father would put me right."

"Lance my father would be delighted to have you work along side him. Why don't you speak him tonight and get his reaction to your plan. The important thing is, what about your position with the British Service?"

"I have already given this a lot of thought and if I resigned my position we would still have enough cash to last us two years, which, by this time, your father will either employ me or sack me" he said laughing.

*

"Personally I think it is a wonderful idea, I wonder if you will get addicted to the wine business. Anything to encourage growth seems to attract the wine farmers except the blight that can ruin the crop of grapes. The big advantage you have Lance would be the wealth of wine growing knowledge that you could glean from all the local farmers"

"I am also very interested in the marketing side of the wine industry."

That evening Anna, Marco and Lance went downstairs and asked Josie and Albert to sit down as they wished to discuss something with them. "Oh! You are not leaving the farm?" said Josie with tears welling in her eyes."

"Not at all, it is more of a proposal." Anna looked at Lance "Anna and I have been talking over our future plans and what I am going to tell you, we have really thought hard about it but it will depend on you both. Albert you said that your health didn't allow you to carry on grafting the cuttings from the six vines to your other stock. How would you like me to help you? We have enough cash to gamble for a year whether or not you decide to employ me after one year. If you agree to our plan, I will resign

179

my service position and work with or for you in the vineyard but this is entirely up to you. If you don't think I would suit you, please say so now and we will stay as we are."

Albert stood up putting his hand out to shake, Lance took Albert's hand and shook it. "Lance I would be delighted to have you work alongside me just think, what a wine industry we can pass on to Marco."

"Firstly I must contact Colonel Snaith and tell him of my decision. I must be straight with him as he has helped me a great deal over the past year."

"Yes Lance you do that, my first job now I have help, is to see what can be salvaged in the large field of vines which the German Officer had ordered his troop to drive their armoured vehicles through. We can prune some of the vines and save the main stems. Fortunately we are coming into the growing season so we are in with a chance. We should also crack on with the grafting using the cuttings from Jacques six vines ready for next years wine. Lance you will sleep well as over the next few weeks, we will be working at least fourteen hours every day." Smiling as he said it.

When the local farmers learned that Lance was going to work for Albert they were very relieved. Rumours had been running around that as older farmers are retiring a conglomerate are going to try and buy the farms to use as building land.

*

Lance was fast asleep in bed when a banging on the bedroom door woke him Albert leaned round the door and he threw a pair of protective trousers on to the bed. "Put these on to protect your legs, coffee is ready and we start work in thirty minutes. Lance was a little dazed, he looked at the clock and saw it was 5.30am. He rolled over hoping to go back to sleep but again Albert banged on the door. He got out of bed and dressed putting on the protective pants and he went downstairs where Albert had a cup of coffee waiting for him. "No breakfast?"

"Breakfast will be ready and you will be fed about nine o'clock but we have a lot of work to get through before then."

They went out of the house into the smaller barn where Albert had put a load of cuttings in a large pail of water. Albert lifted a large bunch out of the water. Come along Lance let us get cracking I will show you the correct way to deal with grafting handing him a very sharp pen knife. They went into the vineyard that the Germans had trashed with their armoured vehicles. Albert selected a live stem and proceeded to show Lance the correct way to carry out a graft. "I must impress on you that you must be very gentle with the stems as they are tender, they must be female." Albert laughed enjoying his own joke. As they were crossing the track to the next field a neighbour was driving past, he shouted. "How is the new boy shaping Albert?" driving away laughing.

*

Later that afternoon Lance was feeling really tired and he realized what Albert said about not having sleepless nights, he was glad when it was time to pack up and go back to the farmhouse. Lance had difficulty in keeping awake while eating his evening meal. Anna jolted him awake telling him that she was pregnant, when they told Josie, she was delighted, "I do hope it is a little girl, don't you Lance?"

"Josie, boy or girl, it will be welcome and loved."

Albert brought in the village newspaper and there was a story about the coroner's inquest on the death of Karl Steiner. The coroner decided that his death was not due to any foul play Karl must have been knocked to the floor by a Boar and attacked before he could get to his feet. It was obvious that more than one animal had attacked him. Karl must have found some truffles and the animals treated him like a thief and that is where the smell of truffles came from.

When Anna finished reading the report she smiled and wondered how the handcuffs and the rope were removed so soon after Karl's death. Albert looked at Anna smiling, "The ladies will be very happy with the result but the authorities will not be altogether satisfied but that is the coroner's decision and that will be regarded as final."

They were all sat round the table enjoying the evening meal prepared by Josie since Anna had told her mother that she was pregnant she would not let Anna do any work at all. Anna was not happy at all being treated like an invalid. Anna argued with her mother saying that child bearing is one of nature's wonders.

*

Albert looked at Lance. "You have worked so hard today and it has been a long day, I will open a bottle of my special red wine." Lance smiled and his mouth started to water at the prospect of having some of the most excellent wine he had ever tasted. Albert toasted the vines they had grafted today and hoping they will produce wine as good as they are drinking. Marco stood up "I will call it Marco's wine." Lance said "Okay it will be labeled Marcos wine if it is as good as this one." Albert said, "Yes that is what we will call it." They all raised their glasses saying "Marcos Wine."

The following morning Lance was up early and waiting for Albert to show in the kitchen and Lance was waiting with the coffee ready. We have a very busy time ahead of us Lance not only are we hoping for a good crop of grapes but we will be very busy keeping on top of the weeds between the rows of vines. Each piece of vegetation is taking goodness and moisture from the soil, they must go, all the moisture and goodness is required by the grapes. They went out to the fields and started dealing with the weeds, just before lunchtime Lance was having trouble with his back and Albert spotted that Lance was in trouble so he went over and gave him a break. Albert took Lance for a walk to a small field this is the soil being prepared to spread around the roots of the vines. "The soil is better if it contains Potassium and Boron to obtain the maximum harvesting of the grapes."

The following week as Albert and Lance walked into the farmhouse, Anna and Josie could see that they were both excited, Lance couldn't contain himself any longer. "75% of the grafts we did are growing and will bear fruit." Josie looked at them both. "That is fantastic you must be pleased with yourselves."

"It is looking good for Marcos wine" laughing as she said it.

Lance was so excited he couldn't stop walking up and down the rows of vines they had grafted. He was so delighted to see the grafts growing and getting stronger each day. This was an achievement he had never experienced before.

The grafts on the vines were watched very carefully ensuring no infection was allowed to settle.

They were delighted when harvest time came around and the red grapes were healthy and fleshy. Albert mentally assessed the amount of good wine they will get from the first fermentation and he was very pleased with their efforts.

Chapter 33

Lance sat back in a comfortable easy chair, he felt as contented as he could ever be. His world was or could be the envy of many a man. He and Anna were so very happy and his in-laws were comfortable with the situation.

Suddenly the phone started ringing he lifted the receiver knowing he will have to call Josie. Hello! The voice at the other end said, "Is it possible that I could speak to Lance at this address?"

"This is Lance speaking, who are you?"

"This is Max, I am delighted to have found you, Bernie's son is almost 14 years of age and he is arranging a Bar- mitzvah and he was hoping we could find and persuade you to attend."

"Where is it being held?"

"At his house in Croydon, Bernie is hoping to get all his friends with whom he had dealings with over the past few years and have become trustworthy friends. It could be the last time we would get together as he is going to retire and go back to Israel to live."

"Max I am unable to give you a definite answer at the moment, what date are we talking?"

"Two weeks time, just ring me Lance and I will arrange everything."

"Cheers Max." Lance just sat back in the chair again to consider the phone call. He will have to discuss it with Anna.

*

Lance sat back turning the invitation over in his mind, perhaps I could tie it in with my visit to Colonel Snaith, that would be ideal. One snag, Anna is getting close to the birth of our second child and I am not sure it will be safe for her to travel or if I want to leave her at that time.

While they were having dinner Lance brought the subject of his visit up. Albert looked at Lance, "Surely you are going to visit Colonel Snaith in view of the help he has given you over the past year."

"That is true Albert and in the case of Bernie, he saved my life on two occasions, in fact you and Josie saved my life. Had you not hid me in the loft of the cottage, I would have been shot the enemy were shooting the airmen they captured." It was decided that he should travel to London alone, Lance was a little uncertain but he realized that this was the only option in fairness to Anna. Lance telephoned Colonel Snaith to make an appointment and the visit to London would coincide with Bernie's invitation. Laughing, Lance turned to Albert, "Will you allow me to take a bottle of your gold to London with me?"

"Of course Lance and I hope they appreciate a bottle of good wine." He had a slight smile playing around his mouth.

"Will you be allowed to bring the jeep back with you?"

"I'm not sure but I am hoping the Colonel will help me in that respect."

"Lance do try and get back for the wine celebration in the village, buyers from all over the world will be here trying to buy the best wines at the cheapest price."

*

There were tears as Lance was leaving to visit London, in fact, he would have preferred to go as a family. He had no difficulty in obtaining a passage on a ship destine for Dover and the fact he had decided to wear his uniform helped, thinking it might help to open doors. He made very good time and he arrived at his hotel in London early evening, he was quite satisfied with the hotel that had been booked for him by the Colonel's office. The first thing he did when he went to his room was to phone Anna, she would like to know that he had arrived safely.

The following morning Lance was up early and enjoyed a good breakfast and as it was a bright clear morning he decided to walk to the Colonel's office.

On entering the building he was directed to the Colonel's office, he knocked on the door and was invited to enter, as he walked in the Colonel got to his feet and greeted Lance as a long lost member of his family. They went into a smaller office and coffee arrived and they sat chatting. Lance turned to the Colonel, "I am going to resign from my position."

"Yes I had heard of your intention on the grapevine."

"Between our selves Lance, I envy your lifestyle as the present time, you have a family and your future is mapped out. I lost my family and my home during the blitz so you can see where I am coming from. Incidentally, if you need a wine taster I'm your man." They both enjoyed a good laugh.

"Have got the jeep with you? You can hold on to it for the time being, the authorities are calling most of them in and eventually all the Jeeps, lorries and various vehicles will go to an auction sale. I will get yours for you at the cheapest price." They shook hands wishing each a happy future knowing they may never meet again.

*

The following day was Bernie's celebration day Lance booked out of his hotel and managed to get a room in a small hotel in Croydon, which, Max had told him about. When Lance booked in, Max had arrived and so once again it was gossip of the happenings over the passed years what each had been doing with their lives. They went to the local tube station and caught a train to the station nearest to Bernie's address, when they found his address and knocked on the door Bernie opened the door and hugged both Max and Lance. Bernie introduced them to his friends and family as true trustworthy friends. During the afternoon Lance asked Bernie to take his son and Max to a separate room, Lance produced a bottle of red wine out of a bag he was clutching. He filled four glasses that was on the table and handed them round and watched their faces as they sipped the wine. Bernie looked at Lance. "This is a wonderful wine Lance it is what I would call a Dessert Wine."

"The amount of wine produced this year is restricted but we are hoping to double our production next year. If you look at the label, it is called Marcos, that is my son's name and he insisted on it being called that name for his future." Bernie told them that he had resigned from the Mossad and he was going to join the family business in Israel. Lance smiled, I resigned from the British Secret Service yesterday and I hope to spend my future helping my father in law to produce this wine. They all raised their glasses saying CHEERS!

Leaving, they all said farewell knowing it is unlikely that they would ever meet again, sad but they left each feeling happy to have met up again.

Chapter 34

Lance was made very welcome on his return home and he was surprised, there was a feeling of electric in the air around the village and there was coloured bunting hanging from the windows. Albert explained it was the celebration of the wine year and all the interested wine buyers will be visiting. "Before the war, they would come from around the world to attend the selection of the wine of the year. This year there is great competition for the wine of the year as some of the wines have been stored hidden for the past five years. Tomorrow the Judges who are from about five different countries. This being the first celebration since the war ended, it should be a good one."

"We have to erect our own stall in the numbered position as shown on a chart on the wall of the Town Hall and we will need to take the small barrel we intend entering into the competition the night before."

"Is it safe to leave wine on the stall the night before?"

"It should be, you will be watching over it until about 2 o'clock in the morning and I will take over from you till the morning." Albert burst out laughing. "Are you kidding me Albert?"

"No, we normally watch over the wine during the night, there are always some people running around trying to steal good wines."

*

The Market opened up and several buyers arrived early. Albert had several barrels of the red wine to sell and he was undecided on the price and he was tempted to sell as ordinary wine to recoup some of the cost of getting his vineyards up and running again. The best red wine, Lance said "No way Albert that wine is brilliant and deserves to be recognized by its price."

"I don't agree with you Lance but today you can have your own modern outlook on sales" The buyers soon started wandering around the stalls more interested in the colouring at present. Several enquired the price of the normal wine and Albert soon sold several of his stock barrels. When they asked the price of Lance's red they walked away, this happened several time and Albert was getting little impatient but Lance refused to budge on his price.

One buyer was interested in the red wine and he made an offer but Lance refused, Albert tried to persuade Lance to lower his price but Lance refused, much to Albert's disgust. Three different buyers offered Lance a lower figure but he still refused. He called the three buyers together and gave them a sample of the red wine, as they sampled it their faces changed and one offered the asking price, one of the others offered a better figure, the third buyer offered Lance a much higher figure if he could buy all the stock. Lance hummed and harred! okay and shook hands on the deal. Albert was staggered at the price Lance got for the red wine he just shrugged his shoulders, I must be getting old and out of touch.

They were just congratulating each other, when a man brought a message saying that Lance was a proud father of a little girl. Albert poured out a drink and they toasted the little girl. "You had better get off Lance I will wind up here but do give Anna my love. We have sold all the stock we wanted to sell and it just remains on the Judges decision on the wine of the year but that will not be announced until later this evening when all the dancing and celebrations take place."

Lance went to the hospital and was guided to the ward where Anna was sat up cuddling the newborn child Lance made no mistake he kissed Anna first before looking at their little girl. He sat looking at Anna and the little girl, how lucky we are Anna. They sat having a cup coffee at peace with the world. He related the story of selling the red wine, she chuckled "I bet Dad was surprised."

"Yes he was, now I am going back to help him dismantle the stall and I will go home and get cleaned up and I should be back in about an hour. Do you want me to bring you anything?"

"No my mother is bringing me things I need and she is going to bring Marco later." He gave her a kiss and left walking on air.

*

Lance went back to the Market Place and they were all dismantling the stalls so Albert was pleased to see Lance return, between them they soon got the stall down and put away. They had to leave the small barrel of red wine on a long table where the judges were working away.

Lance went home to get cleaned up and he had meal and he decided to take Marco to the hospital with him and if Josie left before him she could take him home. Marco was looking forward to meeting new sister and Anna was looking forward to seeing Marco again. Marco was delighted when Lance told him about selling the red wine. "I told you Marcos was the name for that wine." They were sat talking to Anna for a couple of hours and Josie turned up bringing the things Anna wanted. "Would you like to go with me to the Market Place and see what is happening Marco, the music should start soon?"

"Yes please grandma." An hour later, Anna kept dozing off. "Would you like me to go and let you sleep?"

"No you just sit there, I'm happy knowing you are sat there." They were sat, not talking just holding hands when Albert came dashing in, he held his arms out, Lance stood up and Albert embraced him. "We have done it we have the wine of the year." He was so excited. "It is the first time in my life and I have spent years growing vines" Albert went dashing off. Anna and Lance just sat looking into each others eyes and they were filling up with tears, they were so happy.

The End

www.ingramcontent.com/pod-product-compliance
Lightning Source LLC
Chambersburg PA
CBHW020610250626
47154CB00004B/1438